Hellfire, Texas

HELLFIRE SERIES

BOOK #1

ELLE JAMES

New York Times & USA Today
Bestselling Author

Dedication

This book is dedicated to the all the dedicated first responders who risk their lives daily to help people and animals when all hell breaks loose! Thank you to the firefighters, paramedics and law enforcement personnel for being there we need you most.

Escape with...

Elle James

        aka Myla Jackson

Author's Note

Visit **ellejames.com** for more
titles and release dates

Also visit her alter-ego Myla Jackson at
mylajackson.com

Chapter 1

The hot July sun beat down on the asphalt road. Shimmering heat waves rose like mirages as Becket Grayson drove the twenty miles home to Coyote Creek Ranch outside of Hellfire, Texas. Wearing only a sweat-damp T-shirt and the fire-retardant pants and boots of a firefighter, he couldn't wait to get home, strip, and dive into the pool. Although he'd have to hose down before he clouded the water with the thick layer of soot covering his body from head to toe.

The Hellfire Volunteer Firefighter Association met the first Saturday of every month for training in firefighting, rescues, and first responder care. Today had been particularly grueling in the late summer swelter. Old Lady Mersen graciously donated her dilapidated barn for structural fire training and rescue.

All thirty volunteers had been on hand to participate. Though hot, the training couldn't have gone better. Each volunteer got a real taste of how fast an old barn would go up in flames, and just how much time they had to rescue any humans or animals inside.

Some had the opportunity to exercise the use of SCBA, self-contained breathing apparatus, the masks and oxygen tanks that allowed them to enter smoke-filled buildings, limiting exposure and damage to their lungs. Other volunteers manned the fire engine and tanker truck, shuttling water from a nearby pond to the portable tank deployed on the ground. They unloaded a total of five tanks onto the barn fire before it was completely extinguished.

With only one tanker truck, the shuttle operation slowed their ability to put out the fire, as the blaze rebuilt each time they ran out of water in the holding pool. They needed at least two tanker trucks in operation to keep the water flowing. As small as the Hellfire community was, the first engine and tanker truck would never have happened without generous donations from everyone in the district *and* a government grant. But, they had an engine that could carry a thousand, and a tanker capable of thirty-five hundred gallons.

Forty-five hundred gallons was better than nothing.

Hot, tired, and satisfied with what he'd learned about combating fire without the advantages of a city fire hydrant and unlimited water supply, Becket had learned one thing that day. Firefighting involved a lot more than he'd ever imagined. As the Fire Chief said, all fires were different, just like people were different. Experience taught you the similarities, but you had to expect the unexpected.

Two miles from his turnoff, Becket could almost taste the ice-cold beer waiting in the fridge and feel the cool water of the ranch swimming pool on his skin.

A puff of dark smoke drifted up from a stalled vehicle on the shoulder of the road ahead. The puff grew into a billowing cloud, rising into the air.

Becket slowed as he neared the disabled vehicle.

A black-haired woman stood in the V of the open driver's door, attempting to push the vehicle off the road. She didn't need to worry about getting it off the road so much as getting herself away from the smoke and fire before the gas tank ignited and blew the car to pieces.

A hundred yards away from the potential disaster, Becket slammed on his brakes, shifted into park, and jumped out of his truck. "Get away from the car!" he yelled, running toward the idiot woman. "Get away before it explodes!"

The woman shot a brief glance back at him before continuing her mission to get the car completely off the road and into the bone-dry grass.

Becket ran up behind her, grabbed her around the middle, and hauled her away from the now-burning vehicle.

"Let go of me!" she screamed, tearing at his hands. "I have to get it off the road."

"Damn it, lady, it's not safe." Not knowing when the tank would ignite, he didn't have time to argue. Becket spun her around, threw her over his shoulder in a fireman's carry, and jogged away from the burning vehicle.

"I have to get it off the road," she said, her voice breaking with each jolt to her gut.

"Leave it where it is. I'll call in the fire department, they'll have the fire out before you know it. In the meantime, that vehicle is dangerous." He didn't stop or put her down until he was back behind his truck.

He set her on her feet, but she darted away from him, running back toward the vehicle, her long, jet-black hair flying out behind her.

Becket lunged, grabbed her arm, and jerked her back. "Are you crazy?"

"I can't leave it in the road," she sobbed. "Don't you see? He'll find it. He'll find me!" She tried prying his fingers free of her arm.

He wasn't letting go.

"The fire will ignite the gas tank. Unless you want to be fried like last year's turkey, you need to stand clear." He held her back to his chest, forcing her to view the fire and the inherent danger.

She sagged against him, her body shaking with the force of her sobs. "I have to hide it."

"Can I trust you to stay put?"

She nodded, her hair falling into her

face.

"I'm making a call to the Hellfire Volunteer Firefighters Association."

Before he finished talking, she was shaking her head. "No. You can't. No one can know I'm here."

"Why?" He settled his hands on her shoulders and was about to turn her to face him when an explosion rocked the ground.

Becket grabbed the woman around the waist.

She yelped and whimpered as Becket ducked behind the tailgate of his pickup, and waited for the debris to settle. Then he slowly rose.

Smoke and fire shot into the air. Where the car had been, now was a raging inferno. Black smoke curled into the sky.

"Sweetheart, I won't have to call 911. In the next fifteen minutes, this place will be surrounded by firefighters."

Her head twisted left and right as she attempted to pry his hands away from her waist. "You're hurting me."

He released her immediately. "The sheriff will want a statement from you."

"No. I can't." Again, she darted

away from him. "I have to get as far away from here as possible."

Becket snagged her arm again and whipped her around. "You can't just leave the scene of a fire. There will be an investigation." He stared down at her, finally getting a look at her. "Do I know you?"

"I don't…" The young woman glanced up, eyes narrowing. She reached up a hand and rubbed some of the soot off his face. Recognition dawned and her eyes grew round. "Becket? Becket Grayson?"

He nodded. "And I know I should know you, but I can't quite put my finger on it."

Her widened eyes filled with tears, and she flung her arms around his neck. "Oh, dear God. Becket!"

He held her, struggling to remember who she was.

Her body trembled, her arms like clamps around his neck.

"Hey." Surprised by her outburst, Becket patted her back. "It's going to be okay."

"No, it's not," she cried into his

7

sweat-dampened shirt, further soaking it with her tears. "No, it's not."

His heart contracted, feeling some of the pain in her voice. "Yes, it is. But you have to start by telling me who you are." He hugged her again, then loosened the arms around his neck and pushed her to arms' length. "Well?"

The cheek she'd rested against his chest was black with soot, her hair wild and tangled. Familiar green eyes, red-rimmed and awash with tears, looked up at him. "You don't remember me." It was a statement, not a question.

"Sorry. You look awfully familiar, but I'm just not making the connection." He smiled gently. "Enlighten me."

"I'm Kinsey Phillips. We used to be neighbors."

His confusion cleared, and he grinned. "Little Kinsey Phillips? The girl who used to hang out with Nash and follow us around the ranch, getting into trouble?"

Sniffling, she nodded.

Becket shook his head and ran his gaze over her from head to toe. "Look at you, all grown up." He chuckled.

"Although, you didn't get much taller."

She straightened to her full height. "No. Sadly, I stopped growing taller when I was thirteen."

"Well, Little Kinsey…" He pulled her into the curve of his arm and faced the burning mess that had been her car. "What brings you back to Hellfire? Please tell me you didn't come to have your car worked on by my brother, Rider. I'm afraid there's no hope for it."

She bit her lip, and the tremors of a few moments before returned. "I didn't know where else to go. But I think I've made a huge mistake."

Her low, intense tone made Becket's fists clench, ready to take on whatever had her so scared. "Why do you say that?"

"He'll find me and make me pay."

"Who will find you?" Becket demanded, turning her to face him again.

She looked up at him, her bottom lip trembling. "My ex-boyfriend."

Kinsey's shuddered, her entire body quaking with the magnitude of what she'd done. She'd made a bid for freedom. If she didn't distance herself from the condemning evidence, all of her efforts to escape the hell she'd lived in for the past year, would be for nothing.

Sirens sounded in the distance, shaking her out of her stupor and spurring her to action. "You can't let them question me." She turned toward the still-burning vehicle. "It's bad enough this is the first place he'll look for me."

"Who is your boyfriend?"

"Ex-boyfriend," Kinsey corrected. "Dillon Massey."

"Name's familiar. Is he from around here?"

Kinsey shook her head, scanning the immediate area. "No, he's from Waco. He played football for Baylor a couple years ago, and he's playing for the Cowboys now."

"Massey, the quarterback?"

"Yes." She nodded, and then grabbed Becket's hands. "Please, you can't let anyone know I'm here. Dillon will make them think I'm crazy, and that I need him to look out for me." Kinsey pulled herself up straight. "I'm not. I've never been more lucid in my life. I had to get away."

Becket frowned. "Why?"

She raised her blouse, exposing the bruises on her ribs. "And there are more. Everywhere most people won't see."

His brows dipping lower, Becket's nostrils flared. "Bastard."

"You have no idea." Kinsey glanced toward the sound of the sirens. "Please. Let me hide. I can't face anyone."

"Who does the car belong to?"

Her jaw tightened. "Me. I'm surprised it got me this far. The thing has barely been driven in over a year."

"Why not?"

"He parked it in his shed and hid the keys. I found them early this morning, while he was passed out drunk."

"When they conduct the investigation, they'll trace the license plates."

She tilted her chin. "I removed them."

"Did you leave a purse with your identification inside the vehicle?"

"No. I didn't bring anything. I knew I'd have to start over with a new name."

"If there's anything left of the Vehicle Identification Number, they can track it through the system."

Glancing at the empty road, the sirens sounding closer, Kinsey touched Becket's arm. "It will take time for them to find the details. By then, I could be halfway across the country. But right now, I can't talk to the sheriff or the firemen. If anyone knows I'm here, that knowledge could find its way into some police database and will allow Dillon to locate me. He has connections with the state police, the district courts, and who knows what other organizations." She shook her head. "I won't go back to him."

"Okay, okay." Becket rounded to the passenger side and opened the door. "Get in."

She scrambled in, hands shaking, her heart beating so fast she was sure it would explode like the car. Kinsey glanced out the back window of the truck. The road was still clear. A curve hid them from view for a little longer. "Hurry."

"On it." Dillon fired up the engine and pulled onto the blacktop, flooring the accelerator. They reached the next curve before the rescue vehicles appeared.

Kinsey collapsed against the seat back, her nerves shot and her stomach roiling. "That was close."

"Sweetheart, you don't know just how close. If emergency vehicles hadn't been coming, I would not have left. As dry as it's been, a fire like that could spread too easily, consuming thousands of acres if left unchecked."

"I'm sorry. I wouldn't have asked you to leave the scene, but I know Dillon. The last time I tried to leave, I was caught because he called the state police and had me hauled home."

"Couldn't you have gone to a hospital and asked for a social worker to verify your injuries?" Becket glanced her way, his brows furrowed in a deep V. "Women's shelters are located all over Dallas."

"I tried." She turned toward the window, her heart hurting, reliving the pain of the beating he'd given her when he'd brought her home. He'd convinced the hospital she'd fallen down the stairs. No one wanted to believe the quarterback of an NFL team would terrorize his girlfriend into submission, beating her whenever he felt like it. "Look, you don't need to be involved in this. If you could take me to the nearest truck stop, I'll hitch a ride."

"Where would you go?"

"Wherever the trucker is going."

He shook his head. "Hitchhiking is dangerous."

Kinsey snorted. "It'd be a cakewalk compared to what I've been through."

Becket sat silent, gripping the steering wheel so tightly his knuckles turned white. "Nash is part of the sheriff's department in Hellfire now. Let me call him."

"No!" She shook her head, violently. "You can't report me to the sheriff's department. I told you. Dillon has friends everywhere, even in the state police and Texas Rangers. He'd have them looking for me. If a report popped up anywhere in the state, they'd notify him immediately."

"When was the last time he saw you?"

"Last night. After he downed a fifth

of whiskey, Dillon gave me the bruises you saw. I'm sure he slept it off by eight this morning. He'll be looking for me. By now, he's got the state police on the lookout for my car. He probably reported it as stolen. I wouldn't be surprised if he puts out a missing person report, claiming I've been kidnapped." Kinsey sighed. "Take me to the truck stop. I won't have you arrested for helping me."

"I'm not taking you to the truck stop."

Kinsey slid the window down a crack and listened. She couldn't hear the sirens anymore. Her pulse slowed and she allowed herself to relax against the back of the seat.

Becket slowed and turned at the gate to the Coyote Creek Ranch.

The entrance was just as she remembered. Rock columns supported the huge arched sign with the name of the ranch burned into the wood. She'd grown up on the much-smaller ranch next door. The only child of older parents, she'd ride her horse to visit the Graysons. She loved Nash and Rider like the brothers she'd never had. Chance had been a wild card, away more than he was there, and Becket…

As a young teen, Kinsey had the biggest crush on Becket, the oldest of the Graysons. She'd loved his longish blond hair and those startling blue eyes. Even now, covered in soot, his eyes were a bright spot of color on an otherwise-blackened face.

"I can't stay here," she said, looking over her shoulder. "Your wife and children don't need me dragging them through whatever Dillon has in store for me. I guarantee, repercussions will be bad."

"Don't worry about the Graysons. Mom and Dad are in Hawaii, celebrating their 40th anniversary. None of us brothers are married, and Lily's too stubborn to find a man to put up with her."

"What?" Kinsey glanced his way. "Not married? Are the women in this area blind? I practically worshipped you as a child."

Becket chuckled. "I remember you following me around when Nash and Rider were busy. Seems you were always there when I brought a girl out to the ranch."

Her cheeks heated. She'd done her darnedest to be in the way of Becket and his girlfriends. She didn't like it when he kissed and hugged on them. In her dreams, she'd been the one he'd fallen in love with and wanted to marry. But that hadn't happened. He'd dated the prom queen and married her soon after graduation.

"I thought you had married."

"Didn't last."

"Why not?"

"It's a long story."

"If I remember, it's a long driveway up to the ranch house."

Becket paused. For a moment, Kinsey thought he was done talking about his life and failed marriage. Then he spoke again. "After college, Briana wanted me to stay and work for one of the big architecture firms in Dallas. I was okay with the job for a while, but I missed the ranch."

"You always loved being outdoors. I can't imagine you stuck in an office."

He nodded. "Dad had a heart attack four years ago."

"I'm sorry to hear that, but I assume he survived, since they're in Hawaii."

Becket smiled. "He did, but he can't work as hard as he used to."

"So, you came home to run the ranch?"

"Yeah." Becket's gaze remained on the curving drive ahead. "Briana didn't want to leave the social scene. We tried the long-distance thing, but she didn't like it. Or rather, the marriage didn't work for her when she found a wealthy replacement for me."

"Wow. That's harsh."

"Eh. It all worked out for the best. We didn't have children, because she wanted to wait. I like it here. I have satellite internet. I telecommute in the evenings on projects for my old firm, so I stay fresh on what's going on in the industry. During the day, I'm a rancher."

"Sounds like you know what you want out of life." Kinsey sighed and rested her head against the window. "I just want to be free of Dillon."

"What about you? You went to Baylor. Did you graduate?"

"I did. With a nursing degree. I worked in pediatric nursing."

"Did you?"

"For a while. Dillon was still at Baylor when I graduated. When he signed on with the Cowboys, he changed. He said I didn't need to work and badgered me into quitting." Kinsey remembered how much she hated staying at home, and how useless she felt. "I loved my job. The kids were great."

Becket stared at the road ahead. "We leave high school with a lot of dreams and expectations."

"I figured I'd be happily married by now with one or two kids." Kinsey snorted.

"Same here." Becket's lips twisted. "We play the hands we're dealt. How long have you put up with the abuse?"

"Too long." Kinsey stared out the window. "The beatings started when he signed on with the NFL. He'd take me to parties. When his teammates paid too much attention to me, he'd get jealous, drink too much, and hit me when we got back to our place."

"Why didn't you leave him then?"

"In the morning, he'd apologize and promise not to do it again." Her lip pulled back in a sneer. "But, he did. Eventually, he stopped taking me to the parties." Her life would have been so different had she left him the first time he hit her. She'd been a fool to believe he would stop.

"Couldn't you have gone to your family?"

"Each time I mentioned leaving, Dillon flew into a rage and threatened to kill me. Then he took away my car. He said it was for my own good. The car was too old, and needed too much work to drive." At first, Kinsey had thought his action was out of concern for her safety. But her checkbook and credit cards disappeared, and he blamed her for being careless, forcing her to live off whatever pittance of cash he gave her. Without a job, she had no income and became a prisoner in Dillon's home. "He told me I was a terrible driver and shouldn't be on the road. That I'd probably end up crashing into someone."

"The man's a dick."

"Tell me about it." Kinsey bit her lip to keep it from trembling. "I think part of the reason he stopped me from driving was that I'd go to visit my parents. Like he was jealous of how much I loved them, and liked spending time at home. By taking away my car, he left me with no way of getting there. Mom and Dad came up to visit me in Dallas when they could, but after they left, Dillon would stomp around the house, sullen and angry. He'd accuse me of being a mama's girl. If I defended myself, he hit me."

"Your parents were good people," Becket said. "I was sorry to hear of the accident."

Tears slipped from Kinsey's eyes. "They were on their way to visit me, since I couldn't go to them. I think they knew I was in trouble."

"Why didn't you tell them what was going on?"

"I was embarrassed, ashamed, and scared. By then, Dillon was my world. I didn't think I had any other alternatives. And he swore he loved me."

"He had a lousy way of showing it," Becket said through tight lips.

She agreed. Along with the physical abuse, Dillon heaped enough mental and verbal abuse on Kinsey, she'd started to believe him.

You're not smart enough to be a nurse. You'll kill a kid with your carelessness, he'd say.

When her parents died, she'd stumbled around in a fog of grief. Dillon coerced her into signing a power of attorney, allowing him to settle their estate. Before she knew what he'd done, he'd sold her parents' property, lock, stock and barrel, without letting her go through any of their things. He'd put the money in his own account, telling her it was a joint account. She never saw any of the money—never had access to the bank.

Several times over the past few months, she had considered leaving him. But with her parents gone, no money to start over, and no one to turn to, she'd hesitated.

Then, a month ago, he'd beaten her so badly she'd been knocked unconscious. When she came to, she knew she had to get out before he killed her. She stole change out of Dillon's drawer, only a little at a time so he wouldn't notice. After a couple weeks, she had enough for a tank of gas.

Dillon settled into a pattern of

drinking, beating her, and passing out. She used the hours he was unconscious to scour the house in search of her keys. She'd begun to despair, thinking he'd thrown them away. Until last night. He'd gone out drinking with his teammates. When he'd arrived home, he'd gone straight to the refrigerator for another beer. He'd forgotten he'd finished off the last bottle the night before and blamed her for drinking the beer. With no beer left in the house, he reached for the whiskey.

With a sickening sense of the inevitable, Kinsey braced herself, but she was never prepared when he started hitting. This time, when he passed out, she'd raided his pockets and the keychain he guarded carefully. On it was the key to her car.

Grabbing the handful of change she'd hoarded, she didn't bother packing clothes, afraid if she took too long, he'd wake before she got her car started and out of the shed.

Heart in her throat, she'd pried open the shed door and climbed into her dusty old vehicle. She'd stuck the key in the ignition, praying it would start. Dillon had charged the battery and started the car the week before, saying it was time to sell it. Hopefully, the battery had retained its charge.

On her second attempt, she pumped the gas pedal and held her breath. The engine groaned, and by some miracle it caught, coughed, and sputtered to life.

Before she could chicken out, before Dillon could stagger through the door and drag her out of the vehicle, she'd shoved the gear shift into reverse and backed out of the shed, scraping her car along the side of Dillon's pristine four-wheel drive pickup, and bounced over the curb onto the street.

She'd made it out, and she wasn't going back.

Chapter 2

Becket drove around behind the house and parked close to the back porch. He wasn't sure who would be at the ranch house.

"I really think this is a bad idea," Kinsey said. "You have a big family. The more people who know where I am, the more likely the information will get leaked."

"You can trust my family. If I tell them to keep mum about you being here, I guarantee they will."

"What are Rider, Chance, and Nash doing these days?"

Becket dropped down from his pickup and rounded to her side, opening the door before answering. "As I mentioned, Rider's into cars. He bought an auto repair shop in Hellfire. He works long hours, so he rarely comes out to the ranch, preferring to stay at his apartment over the shop. When he doesn't have his head under a hood, he's pretty handy at day trading. But if you ask him, he'll tell you he prefers working with his hands, restoring vintage cars and motorcycles."

"He always did like tinkering with the equipment." Kinsey grinned. "Your father would get so mad when he'd come looking for his chainsaw, tractor, or riding lawn mower. Rider usually had them torn into pieces. He always managed to put them back together, though."

"And they ran better." Becket grabbed her around the waist and swung her to the ground.

Kinsey's face blanched and she swayed, bracing a hand on his chest.

Becket slipped an arm around her and held Kinsey against him. "Are you all right?"

"Yeah." She gave him a wan smile. "Just a little dizzy. What is Chance up to?"

"He's one of the few full-time firefighters and EMTs at the Hellfire Fire Department."

She glanced up at him. "They have a full-time staff now? Wasn't it all volunteer?"

"The town's population has grown. People are moving out of the cities, wanting a simpler life away from the rat race."

"Yeah, but that much?"

"You'd be surprised. In the last year, we've added a new grocery store, a small shopping center, a florist, and two new restaurants." He chuckled and raised an eyebrow. "We even have a massage parlor."

"Hellfire's really moving up in the world to afford a full-time fire department."

"We couldn't afford a huge full-time staff, so we make do with volunteers, especially when fighting grass fires and structural fires in out of the way places."

"Like the Coyote Creek Ranch."

"Exactly."

"And you're a volunteer? Or are you full-time, along with full-time ranching and part-time architecture?"

He shook his head. "A volunteer. I have my hands full enough with the ranch and my firm."

"Then why volunteer?"

"Partly for the training, but mostly to help others. If a fire spreads out of control, the destruction could make it to the ranch. Rather help nip the blaze in the bud before it gets too big to contain."

Her gaze swept over him, lingering

on his chest. "I take it you were training today."

"What was your first clue?"

"Hmmm." She held up her hands, smudged black from touching him. "I'd say the fine layer of soot was a dead giveaway."

"You got it right." He took her hand and led her toward the house. "We were practicing barn fires."

Her hand squeezed his. "Sounds hot. And dangerous."

"It was."

"What about your sister, Lily? Does she still live at home?"

"She does. She's a kindergarten teacher in Hellfire. During the summer, she hires out as an au pair and travels around the world with rich families, watching their kids."

"Where'd she go this summer?"

"She hasn't gone yet. Lily is in Dallas today, purchasing clothes and supplies for her trip to Guatemala to babysit for a rich Spanish banana farmer, who wants her to teach his children English while he and his wife visit relatives in Madrid."

"Which leaves Senor Sanchez and

his wife, Margarita." Kinsey climbed the steps to the porch. "Margarita made the best *tamales*."

"She's still here, and she still makes great *tamales*." Becket opened the back door and held it for Kinsey. "If we're lucky, we'll be served *sopapillas* when they return from San Antonio. Margarita always had a soft spot for you."

Kinsey's eyes clouded with tears as she stepped across the threshold into the huge kitchen. "I remember spending so many hours in here, eating lunch and helping her make cookies. I'm sure your parents got tired of feeding me."

"My parents love kids. Hell, they had five of us. What was one more? They probably thought you were one of us."

"I miss my folks."

The sadness in her eyes cut straight through Becket's heart. "I'm sorry for your loss. The good news is that when my father heard their land went up for sale, he bought it. But, they haven't had time to do anything with the house or its contents. The place probably looks the same as the last time you visited. With an inch of fine Texas dust."

"I didn't know that. That entire time right after their accident was a blur. Dillon never visited my family with me, but he *did* take me to the funeral and insisted on me giving him power of attorney to handle their estate. He told me the money from the sale of my parent's place went into paying off the mortgage, and other debts they'd incurred. There wasn't much left. He said he put the remainder in a joint checking account, but he never gave me access." Tears slipped down her cheeks, and she brushed them away. "I never had a chance to go through my parents' things."

Becket touched her arm. "We can go see the house while you're here, if you like."

Squaring her shoulders, Kinsey nodded. "I'd like that." She glanced around the kitchen, drawing in a deep breath. "Smells like chocolate chip cookies." Again, her eyes filled.

"I'm sure Margarita left some in the cookie jar. You're welcome to them."

She gave him a watery smile. "Thank you for taking me in. I don't know what else I would have done."

Becket pulled her into his arms.

"Don't worry. Dillon won't find you here. And if he does, he'll have to go through me, my brothers, my sister, Pedro, and Margarita to get to you."

Kinsey laughed, her voice shaky. "And if you and your brothers aren't scary enough, I saw Lily really mad when she was only ten years old. She scared me back then."

The smile on Kinsey's face was the one Becket remembered from when she'd been a leggy fifteen-year-old: happy, carefree, and full of hopes and dreams for the future. It killed him that Kinsey's boyfriend had physically and mentally abused her into this insecure, frightened woman with bruises and scratches all over her body. "Lily doesn't put up with crap," Becket said. "I have a feeling she'd call bullshit on Dillon for what he did. I'll bet we have to hold her back from going after the bastard." Like Becket wanted to do. But to do that, he'd have to act against her wishes and reveal where Kinsey was hiding.

Becket couldn't let the bastard get away with what he'd done. "I'm calling Nash."

Kinsey touched his arm. "Please, don't. If he's still living here, he'll be home soon enough. We can talk to him then."

"I want him to keep an eye out for Dillon. If he shows up in town, I want to know immediately."

"Dillon won't be here that soon. My parents have been dead for a while. Hopefully, he won't think I have anything to come back here for."

"Why *did* you come back?" Becket held up a hand. "Not that I want you to leave already, but you don't have blood relatives here."

"I don't know." She lifted a shoulder. "I just kind-of headed out of Dallas. I had nowhere else to go. I wasn't even sure what I'd do next. I ended up here." She twisted the hem of her T-shirt. "I don't have any money. I would have run out of gas soon, anyway, and as far as I'm concerned, I'm glad the car burned. A fire might be the best way of hiding it, short of pushing the wreck into a ravine."

Not hardly. "Unfortunately, someone is bound to put together the make and model with the one Dillon will report stolen."

Kinsey inhaled deeply and let it out. "I'll be gone by then."

He tensed. "How? You just said you have no money. Hell, if your clothes were in that car, they're gone, too."

She laughed, the sound cold, flat, and without mirth. "I got away with only the clothes on my back. I didn't dare take the time to pack anything. I brought the only thing I cared about." Kinsey removed a wrinkled photo from the back pocket of her jeans and held it out.

Becket took the tattered, faded photograph. "A photo of your parents. I would think you would have inherited all of their photos."

"Dillon claimed the will said everything was to be sold. I don't remember much from the weeks following the funeral. I think he was glad when they died. Then I was all alone in the world. He didn't have to be nice anymore. I didn't have anyone who gave a damn about me, and he knew it."

Becket didn't have anything to say that could take away the hurt and pain in Kinsey's eyes. Instead, he opened his arms.

Kinsey leaned into him, burying her face against his dirty, soot-stained, smelly shirt.

She didn't seem to mind. Her arms slipped around his waist and she hugged him, clinging to him as though she might be torn away if she loosened her hold. After a while, even Becket couldn't stand his own smoky smell. "Look, let's get cleaned up and make a plan of attack for when the others get home. We have to be ready to field their questions, because I know they'll have some. I'll call Rider and have him come to the ranch for dinner tonight, as well. Since he lives in town, he might have a better vantage point, should Dillon show up."

"I don't want to be a bother."

"Too late for that." He kissed her forehead, the touch making his lips tingle. This was the teen who had followed him around like a loyal puppy. Only, she wasn't a teen anymore. She was a beautiful young woman with all the right curves and long, silky hair a man liked to sink his hands into and tug until she tilted her chin to accept a real kiss.

A groan started up Becket's throat, and he swallowed hard to keep it from being voiced.

"Is something wrong?" Kinsey blinked up at him.

"No. I'm just thinking. Lily is a lot taller, but she might have some clothes you could borrow."

"I can wait until she returns from Dallas to ask her."

"She might decide to stay in Dallas. I'm sure she won't mind." He took her hand, strode through the kitchen, and into the front foyer of the century-old two-story ranch house. "Come on, you can have Rider's room since he's not using it."

Becket led her up the stairs and across the upper landing, stopping to open a door. "Make yourself at home. I'll bring you some clothes." The room was large, with mahogany furniture and a tasteful navy, cream, and brown comforter spread across the queen-size bed.

He moved down the hallway to another door. "I'm in the room next to you, if you need anything, and the bathroom is across the hallway from me." He pushed open the door to a modest bathroom with two vanity sinks and a separate room for the shower and toilet. "Towels, shampoo, and soap are in the cabinet."

"You should go first."

"There's a shower in the master suite I can use. I'll lay Lily's clothes on the vanity in here. Give me a few minutes' head start. I don't want to touch anything until I scrub off the black." He grinned, white teeth standing out in his soot-covered face.

Kinsey ducked into the bathroom and closed the door behind her, leaving it unlocked. She loaded her arms with a towel, washcloth, shampoo, and soap and entered the inner bathroom to find a tub-shower combination. Since she guessed Becket would take longer to wash the soot off his body, Kinsey filled the tub and dropped a fragrant bath oil bead she'd found in the cabinet into the water. Locking the inner door, she slipped out of her smoky dirty jeans, shirt, bra, and panties. A lump formed in her throat. The pathetic pile of clothes was all the worldly goods she possessed.

How would she start over if she

didn't have money, clothes to interview in, or a vehicle to get her to and from a job? She couldn't rely on the Graysons forever. Her stay at the Coyote Creek Ranch could only be temporary.

Maybe she could go to San Antonio or Houston, and find a women's shelter willing to take her in. Of course, first she'd have to get to there. Hitchhiking was dangerous, but her only choice with no money for food or transportation.

All the possibilities tumbled through her thoughts, making her body tense and her belly knot with the magnitude of what she'd done. No matter what, she vowed not to go back to Dillon. Her body and mind couldn't take any more of his abuse.

Forcing the trauma of the last twenty-four hours out of her system, she settled into the warmth of the tub, allowing the water and the heavenly scent to soothe her ravaged soul. She leaned back and relaxed, letting the warm water loosen her muscles.

Her mind drifted to Becket. He was every bit as handsome as he'd been when she was a kid. Even more so. His shoulders had broadened, and his face had weathered with the sun and age. Those blue eyes were the same, and his crisp blond hair had grown longer.

His wife had been a fool, leaving him for another man.

Kinsey had to admit, she still carried a spark of her teenage crush inside. But having just left a really bad relationship, she was in no shape to start a new one.

A wash of dread threatened to spoil her soak in the tub.

Dillon wouldn't let her go easily. He'd find a way to make her look unhinged, claim that she cried wolf about abuse. He had the money and the connections to make discredit her. Kinsey's hand sluiced through the water, landing on her bruised rib. She winced, her resolve strengthening.

She refused to go back. Dillon might love her in his twisted, sick way, but she wasn't strong enough to fend off his blows. One day, he might swing a little too hard and kill her. Whatever love she'd had for him had died over the past year. She was glad she hadn't married the man, or had children with him. Her heart pinched.

Kinsey couldn't imagine a child brought up in such an abusive environment. Now that she was away from him, she could see all the damage he'd done. It would be a long time before she trusted another man claiming to love her.

When the water began to cool, she pulled the plug and stood in the tub, turned on the shower, and washed her thick black hair. She'd have it cut soon. Short. Dillon hated short hair on women. Kinsey had kept her hair shoulder-length through high school and grew it out in college, more because she didn't have time to find a good stylist.

Dillon had loved running his hands through its length. Then, when the beatings began, he used her hair to control her, grabbing it and yanking her around, slamming her into the walls and furniture.

If she couldn't get it cut soon, she'd hack it off herself. Kinsey would never let a man use it against her again.

She dried off, wrapped the towel around her body, and opened the door.

Becket stood in the room with the sink, placing a handful of clothes on the vanity. He wore only a pair of jeans. Scrubbed free of the layer of black, he looked more like the old Becket she remembered. Darkly tanned skin from hours working shirtless in the sun, his blond hair slicked back, curling on the ends around his broad shoulders, he was the kind of handsome that took a girl's breath away.

At this moment, Kinsey struggled to breathe.

Becket smiled. "I hope some of this will fit."

Her pulse fluttered, and her core tightened at the way his presence filled a room. Sure, Dillon was an NFL quarterback. Although his body was rock solid and muscular, she'd quit thinking of him as attractive. He'd used his strength to inflict harm on her.

Becket's warm smile and blue eyes didn't scare her like Dillon's dark eyes and intimidating glare. "Thank you."

His smile fading, Becket stepped closer.

Kinsey backed away, clutching the towel tighter.

His jaw tight, Becket stopped. "I'm

sorry. I just noticed the bruises on your shoulders. He really did a number on you, didn't he?"

She nodded, pain fading in a surprising flare of desire. Naked beneath the towel, she only had to open it toward him. But who would want a woman with ugly red marks and deep purple bruises all over her body?

Becket's head moved back and forth slowly. "We need to get you to the clinic in Hellfire and have them record the bruises. You'll need that kind of documentation when you file for a restraining order."

Her grip on the towel tightened. "I told you, I don't want him to know I'm here."

"Sweetheart, you can't run forever. Dillon doesn't own everyone in the state. I know a good attorney in town. She can help you, and she'll keep your case confidential."

Kinsey's first instinct was to stay beneath the radar. Dillon couldn't find her. But Becket was right. She had to make sure Dillon never got his hands on her again. "Okay. But only the lawyer."

He winced. "She might want you to

visit the clinic in town."

Her stomach roiled. Having only just escaped, she didn't want to be dragged back into Dillon's control. "I don't know."

Becket gave her a brief smile. "Let's take it one step at a time. Get dressed. We'll go see Natalie."

"Natalie?"

"Natalie Rhoades. The attorney." Becket backed out of the bathroom, pulling the door closed as he retreated. "Can you be ready in ten minutes?"

"I can be ready in five."

Becket's smile broadened. "That's the Kinsey I remember. Always ready to go on her next adventure." He winked and left her in the bathroom.

Kinsey snorted. She would be ready in five minutes because she didn't have a blow dryer or makeup. Not that she normally did much with her hair. Besides, it took too long to dry it.

She dressed quickly in the clothing Becket provided. Apparently, Lily had grown quite a bit from the ten-year-old Kinsey remembered. The jeans were four inches too long and loose around her waist and hips. Thankfully, the belt Becket brought helped keep them from falling off. Rolling the hem of the legs kept her from tripping over them. The shirt was long, but tight across her breasts. Though petite, Kinsey had an ample bosom, one of the things that had attracted Dillon in the first place. If she could change them, she would. He'd pinched, bit, and squeezed them until she'd wished she were flat-chested, like in her early teens.

After she tied the tails of the blouse at her waist and rolled up the sleeves to her wrists, she gathered her dirty clothes and stepped out of the bathroom.

Becket stood in the hallway, a telephone receiver against his ear. He nodded to acknowledge her, but continued his conversation. "We'll be there in twenty minutes. Thanks for seeing us on short notice." When he hung up, he swept his gaze over her from head to toe.

Kinsey's body warmed.

"We definitely have to find clothes that fit you better. Lily's a lot taller."

"I'm just grateful I have clothes. Is it possible to put mine in the washer before we leave?"

"Absolutely." He showed her to the laundry room off the other end of the kitchen.

Kinsey settled her jeans and T-shirt in the tub, added detergent from a box on a shelf, and switched on the washer. She turned to leave and stopped short.

Becket was leaning against the doorframe, his gaze on her. "We'll pick up some items in town."

"I don't have any money," Kinsey said. "And I won't accept charity. The clothes I'm wearing now are a loan."

"You have to have something that fits. Let me loan you some money until you're on your feet."

Kinsey frowned. She didn't like being beholden to anyone, but she didn't have a choice. "Is there anything I can do around the ranch? I'll earn my keep."

"I really can afford to spare a few dollars, but if it makes you feel better, you can help me with some of the ranch chores."

"Thanks." She nodded, tension easing from her body. "I don't want to be a problem, or mooch off you and your family."

"Darlin', you're not a problem. Seems your ex-boyfriend is the issue here."

"Yeah, but by coming here, he becomes your problem, as well as mine."

Becket raised his hand. "Don't. I'll take my chances."

"What about the rest of your family?"

"Ask them tonight, when they come home."

Kinsey chewed on her bottom lip. Becket had a lot of siblings. That meant a lot of people would know her secret. Having grown up with them, she knew they could be trusted. "Fair enough."

"Now, let's go see Natalie."

She followed Becket to the back door.

Before opening it, he reached for his cowboy hat on the rack nailed to the wall. He settled it onto his head before reaching for another. "This one is my mother's, and she won't mind if you use it. It'll hide part of your features when we're going through town."

She wound her hair up on top of her head and settled the hat over it. With the different clothes and the hat, Kinsey relaxed a little. Hopefully, Dillon wouldn't recognize her if he'd managed to follow her to Hellfire.

Chapter 3

Twenty minutes later, Kinsey stood in Natalie Rhoades' office. Becket waited outside while she showed Natalie the bruises Dillon had inflicted.

Natalie's brows dipped into a low V over the bridge of her nose as she snapped pictures with a camera. "The man should be shot. I'll have my contacts in Dallas file the paperwork for a restraining order before the close of business today. They will have them served today or tomorrow."

"Can he trace the documents back to Hellfire?"

"There is a possibility. You need to go to the clinic and have a doctor examine you, preferably with a female police officer there to record the evidence." When Kinsey started to shake her head, Natalie held up a staying hand. "You have to file charges eventually. Otherwise, his attack will never go on his record. If you don't take action for you, you should do it for any other woman he decides to beat up. The man is a

47

monster."

"What if it was just me who brought out the worst in him?" Kinsey asked. "He didn't start beating me until well after we'd been living together for a year."

"When did you move in with him?" Natalie asked.

"Two years ago." And, to think, she'd been happy to have the love and attention of a handsome NFL football player.

"When did he start hitting you?"

"Things got tense after a party with his teammates. But they didn't get really bad until right after my parents were killed in a car accident, a year ago."

"Do you have any other family?" the lawyer asked.

Kinsey shook her head. "I was an only child of parents who were only children. Their deaths left me alone. Things were getting tense during the football season. I think the pressure of the games got to him. And coming home to me made him even more stressed."

Natalie reached for one of Kinsey's hands. "No amount of stress excuses *anyone* from beating another human. You did the right thing by leaving. Now, let me help you by filing that restraining order."

"I can't pay you." Kinsey held out her hands, palms up. "I have nothing."

"The filing's on me. Gratis." Natalie smiled. "Say the word, and I could sue him for damages. You'd have a good case."

Kinsey shook her head. "I don't want anything from Dillon."

"At the very least, you need enough to get started."

Kinsey chewed on her bottom lip. "I just want to be done with Dillon, once and for all." She didn't think suing for damages would be as simple as filing a restraining order. Dillon held on tight to what he believed was his property. She sighed. "I don't want to be a burden to the Graysons."

Natalie laughed. "They have so many siblings, they won't notice another person among them. Besides, Becket's looking out for you. He's all heart, the big softy." The lawyer leaned closer. "But don't tell him I said so. He'd deny that label to his grave." She led Kinsey to the door and opened it.

Becket paced the carpet in front of the receptionist's desk. When he turned and spotted them, he strode across the floor and stopped in front of Kinsey. "Well?"

"She's got a good case against Mr. Massey," Natalie said. "We need to get her to the clinic for a thorough evaluation and make sure no other injuries we can't see exist. Plus, they'll do a better job of medically documenting than I can. She'll need a female law officer to assist."

Becket's lips quirked. "I'm glad you had more luck convincing her than I did."

"I'll go," Kinsey said. "If, by revealing what happened to me, I can save another woman from Dillon's abuse, I have to do this." She trembled and crossed her arms over her middle. "Like you said, I can't run forever."

"And you're surrounded by people who know and love you, here in Hellfire," Natalie added with a brief touch to her arm.

Kinsey wasn't so sure about the love part, but many of the people in Hellfire knew her from when she grew up there. Stuffing her hair into her hat, she pulled the brim down low on her forehead. Even though she'd agreed to go to the clinic, the longer Dillon took to find her, the better. The restraining order would take time to make it through the channels and be served to Dillon. Until then, she wasn't advertising the fact she was back in Hellfire.

An hour later, after the humiliation of showing her body to members of the Hellfire Clinic staff and having pictures taken of parts she hadn't exposed in public since she was an infant, Kinsey was both physically and emotionally drained. Dressed in the oversized clothes again with her hair hidden in the cowboy hat, she left the clinic with Becket. "Could we go back to the ranch?" she asked, pulling the hat brim low as they drove through town.

"After one more stop to get you some clothes."

"Only if we go to a resale shop. I don't know when I can pay you back, and I don't want to start a new life in debt."

"Okay." Becket doubled back and turned off Main Street onto one of the side streets, stopping in front of a building. The sign read **WOMEN'S SHELTER THRIFT SHOP**. "I'd rather take you to one of the other shops on Main Street."

"This is perfect."

Becket circled the truck and opened her door.

She hesitated, needing to be clear about this purchase. "I'll pay back every dollar, as soon as I get a job. I promise."

"You don't have to." Becket held out his hand.

Kinsey laid her hand in his. "Maybe not, but I will." His blue-eyed gaze captured hers as she stepped down from the truck. She missed the running board and fell into Becket's arms.

He caught her and held her against his chest until she could get her feet under her. "Are you okay?"

A dull ache shot through her middle. Her heart beat so hard against her ribs, she couldn't catch her breath. Kinsey rested her hands against Becket's chest, her cheeks heating. "I'm sorry, I'm so clumsy."

"No, you're fine. Falling happens to everyone." His voice was soft, low, and rumbled in his chest, warming her where her breasts pressed against him.

Falling is a very bad idea. She reminded

herself she was just getting out of a relationship. Becket was a good-looking man. If she got involved with him—which she wouldn't—he'd be a rebound relationship. Not something that would last. Realizing they were far too close to each other, she pushed against him. "I'll hurry."

"Take your time and get all you need."

Kinsey selected two pairs of jeans, a couple pairs of shorts, several blouses and T-shirts and headed for a dressing room in the back corner. The items fit a lot better than those borrowed from Lily's closet. When she'd finished trying them on, she opened the door to the dressing room.

Becket was there with two dresses and a pair of red cowboy boots.

"What are those for?" she asked, frowning. "I have all I need."

"If you want to interview for jobs, you'll need something a little dressier than jeans." He handed her a hunter green dress. "This one matches your eyes." He also gave her a soft gray business suit jacket and skirt. "I guessed on the sizes."

Touched by his thoughtfulness,

Kinsey handed him the jeans and shirts and stepped back into the dressing room with the dress and suit. She *would* need dressy clothes for interviewing. The sooner she found a job, the sooner she'd have money to pay back Becket.

The dress and suit fit perfectly. For guessing, Becket was right on. Back in her oversized clothes, she emerged from the dressing room, selected a nightgown to add to the pile and joined Becket at the checkout counter, where he paid for her purchases. Thankfully, the total wasn't horrible. Glad she'd insisted on the thrift shop, she took the bag of gently used items and left, feeling a little more hopeful about starting over. "Thank you, Becket. I'll keep a total of what I owe you, and I'll pay you back as soon as possible."

"Take your time. You've been through a lot." He took the bag from her and settled it on the back seat. "I'm just happy you came to us."

Kinsey climbed into the truck and waited for Becket to slip into the driver's seat. "About that…"

"About what?"

"That thrift shop supports a women's shelter. I didn't know Hellfire had one."

"Along with the growth in population, there was an increase in battered women. The Ladies Aide Society set one up for the county."

Though she didn't relish the idea, she had to offer it to Becket. "Rather than inconveniencing you and your family, I should go to the shelter."

"No."

The one word was spoken with such finality, Kinsey was hesitant to continue. But she did, determined not to be a burden on the Graysons. "It would make more sense than sponging off you."

"You're not inconveniencing or sponging off us. You are part of the family." He reached across the seat and gripped her hand. "If Dillon comes looking, who will protect you?"

"Surely, the shelter has security measures in place."

"I don't trust they would be good enough. Tell you what, let the rest of the family weigh in. If they want you to stay, this topic won't be brought up again. Okay?"

Kinsey stared at where their hands connected. Electric currents like she hadn't felt in so long coursed through her arm, into her chest, and lower. Staying with Becket Grayson was a terrible idea. That crush she'd had on him so many years ago hadn't gone away completely. In fact, the feelings were getting stronger the more she was with him.

The thought of Dillon finding her raised gooseflesh on her skin. She would feel better protected with the Graysons than on her own with strangers at the shelter.

"Okay." She aimed a hard glance his way. "But if they want me to go, I'm going. No argument."

He let go of her hand and turned the key in the ignition. "No argument." Becket's lips quirked upward on the sides. "I've even invited Rider to the house to have a say. He's also in a position to keep an eye and ear open for strangers in town. His shop is just off Main Street, but the diner is right next door. He sees just about everyone who comes in and out."

Back at the ranch, Becket left Kinsey in the laundry room and retreated to the barn where he mucked the soiled shavings from the stalls, and then fed and watered the horses, cattle, and chickens. He'd needed the space. After spending the morning with Kinsey, he was feeling things he shouldn't. Every time he touched her, he couldn't deny the jolt of fire that raced through his system, igniting desire he'd long thought buried with his divorce.

Kinsey had grown into a beautiful young woman. Though he could still see the same girl inside her, she was mature now, all the curves filled in and stunning. Why did she have to grow up? Perhaps he should have taken her to the women's shelter. At least there, she would have a place to stay and get back on her feet. He wouldn't be tempted by the woman who'd been like a kid sister.

No. Becket would have been on edge the entire time, wondering if Dillon would find her there and take her back to Dallas and her life of hell.

He had to control his increasing

desire and be the big brother, even if what he felt was anything but brotherly. Add the fact she was just getting out of an abusive relationship, and he would be in way over his head. Kinsey needed time to recover.

He was filling a trough with water in one of the pastures that led off the corner of the barn when Kinsey joined him, wearing Lily's jeans tucked into the bright red cowboy boots. Because of her petite body, she looked like a little girl in big-girl clothes. Vulnerable and beautiful. The sexy full lips and the swell of her breasts made Becket reevaluate the little-girl image. He found himself wanting to touch his mouth to hers to ascertain whether her lips were as soft and responsive as they appeared.

She stuck her hands in her back pockets and rocked on her heels. "Could I help you with something?"

Her movement strained the fabric over her breasts.

Becket groaned. *You could go away and let my life return to normal.*

"Everything's covered," he said. "All I had left was filling the trough."

"What time does your family come

home?"

"It varies. They should all be here after seven."

"If you don't mind, I can cook dinner."

"You don't have to cook. I can have Chance pick up something at the diner in town."

"I don't mind. I'm quite good at it." She laughed. "I had to be, to please Dillon."

"Well, you don't have to cook for us. We're pretty good at fending for ourselves."

"I noticed some chicken in the freezer. I could thaw it out and make a big pot of chicken and dumplings."

Becket's mouth watered. "Margarita usually does the cooking, but with her and Pedro visiting family in San Antonio, and Mom and Dad in Hawaii, we've been eating out or making pancakes for dinner."

Kinsey grinned. "Then let me do the cooking tonight."

"You don't have to twist my arm." He winked. "When do you have to start?"

"Soon."

"I'll help." He turned off the hose and wiped his wet hands on his jeans.

Kinsey's brows puckered. "I'm not making pancakes."

"I know." He closed the barn door and waved his hand toward the house. "After you."

As they walked, Becket admitted, "I've helped Margarita in the kitchen a time or two. Lately, I've been too busy, and she shoos me out. Since I took the day off of mending fences and mowing fields to fight fires, I can help out."

"Okay. But maybe after you shower again." Kinsey laughed, waving a hand in front of her nose. "You smell."

Becket laughed, too. "I could always trust you to call it as it is." Not only was she beautiful, she was the same Kinsey he remembered inside—honest, funny, and caring.

If he ever ran into Dillon, he'd wring the man's neck. Anyone who'd hurt this woman was one sick bastard.

Kinsey got the chicken boiling with the onions, carrots, celery, and broth, and Becket pulled out the other ingredients and supplies needed to roll out the dough for dumplings.

For such a large kitchen, the space seemed to shrink with Becket in it. Every time she turned around, Kinsey bumped into him. She rinsed a knife in the sink and dried it off. Then she turned, and Becket was right there, reaching over her head for something in the cabinet behind her.

"Sorry," he said, his breath warm in her hair. "I thought we could use something to drink. It's getting kind of…" he paused with the glass in his hand, "…hot in here."

Kinsey's heated cheeks and body were proof of that. But the air conditioning did nothing to quench the fire inside. "Umm, do you know how to make the dumplings?"

"I believe I have everything you want on the counter."

Everything I want? Kinsey could think of other things besides flour and rolling pins. "Okay, I can roll out the dough."

"Show me what to do, and I'll do it." Becket stood where he was without moving, blocking her escape.

Her pulse humming through her body, Kinsey was tempted to lean into him.

But having escaped one man, she didn't think she was ready to start anything with another—no matter how tempting Becket was. "You could start by letting me get past you."

He tilted his head, a smile playing across his lips. "You're not like I remembered."

Neither are you. "Not the skinny kid following you and your brothers all over the ranch?"

"No." His gaze seared a path down her length. "Not the gangly teen. You've filled out in all the right places."

Her body tingled everywhere his glance lingered, and Kinsey hiked her brows. "Sounds like a line."

"No line. Just the truth." He stepped back and waved to the counter with the ingredients for dumplings. "Show me."

Hands trembling, she measured flour and shortening into a bowl and cut it together, then added water. Once she had it all mixed into a big, doughy ball, she turned to Becket. "If you want to help, you can sprinkle flour on the pastry sheet."

He grabbed a handful of flour and

dusted the sheet. "Like this?" When he finished, he tossed some at her.

It hit her square in the face, spreading white powder all over her nose and cheeks. She blinked for several seconds, then nodded calmly and set the round ball of dough on the pastry sheet. Without remarking on the flour in the face, she dipped her fingers into the flour canister. "When you roll out the dough, you have to dust your rolling pin to keep it from sticking." She sprinkled the flour on the rolling pin, and then tossed some at Becket's face. Her shot missed and landed in his hair, sliding down the side of his head into his ear. He looked so ludicrous, the sight made Kinsey giggle.

He nodded. Straight-faced. "I see. Perhaps we should roll out the dough." Becket stepped closer, took the pin from her, and rolled it across the big ball, barely making a dent.

"You have to be firm with it." Kinsey laid her hands over his, pressed the pin into the pastry, and rolled it flatter. He smelled good, like soap, aftershave, and male. The white flour in his hair made him more approachable, fun-loving, and somehow younger than the oldest Grayson brother. He'd changed—grown older, matured, and become the responsible, potential head of the family in the intervening years—and she liked him even more than she had as that young teen. If only she hadn't just come from the disaster of Dillon.

Flour hit her smack in the face again. Kinsey wiped at the white stuff and sneezed. "Hey. We were even up to that point. Now it's game on." She grabbed a handful and threw. This time her aim was true, and the bulk of the flour hit him in the face.

Kinsey clapped her hands and giggled. "Ha! Gotcha that time."

"You realize that no good aim goes unpunished." Another puff of flour exploded on her forehead.

"You're making a mess of the kitchen," she warned, opening a cabinet door to block his next assault. "Someone has to clean this up." Kinsey let down her guard for a second. More flour exploded on her shoulder. "That's it. Gloves come off.

It's time for some payback."

This time, when she saw him scoop a handful of flour, Kinsey ran.

Laughing, Becket gave chase.

Kinsey dodged him, running around the kitchen island.

Becket ran after her, and then switched directions, ending up in front of her.

In her attempt to stop, Kinsey skidded, her feet slipping on the flour coating the floor. "Whoa." She teetered, and then fell forward.

Fortunately, Becket was there to catch her, pulling her into his arms before she hit the floor.

With Becket's arms around her, she froze, her breath catching in her lungs. Her breasts pressed against his chest. She'd never felt more excited and confused as at that moment in Becket's arms. With all her heart, she wished she could stay right where she was, with his strong arms wrapped tightly around her. Safe, secure, and cared for. This was how love was supposed to be. Not controlling, demanding, and painful.

Becket's gaze burned into hers.

The look made her want things she hadn't wanted in so long. His mouth was only a couple inches away. Her attention shifted to his full, sexy lips.

"You should laugh more," he said, his head tipping toward her.

"I needed a reason to laugh." She stared at his face dotted with flour, her lips curling. "Do you know how ridiculous you look?" She reached up and brushed white powder from his brow, her fingers sliding across his cheek and down to his lips, her gaze following.

"Do you know how sexy you are?" he asked, his voice low and gravely.

Kinsey laughed, feeling surprisingly lighthearted. "Covered in flour?"

"Yeah. Your eyes sparkle, and your mouth makes the prettiest shape when you smile." He bent closer.

Breath catching in her throat, Kinsey leaned closer, her lips tingling in anticipation of contact with his.

"Are we interrupting something? Or did the pantry explode?" a female voice said.

The moment shattered. And Kinsey

sucked in a steadying breath.

Becket straightened, holding onto Kinsey until she was steady on her feet.

Her knees wobbled, but she could stand alone. She pushed away from his arms and turned toward the door.

Lily, Rider, Chance, and Nash stepped into the kitchen.

"So, where's the fire?" Chance asked.

"Yeah, why the family meeting?" Nash crossed his arms over his chest, his brows dipping.

"And…" Rider waved a hand in her direction. "Who's the girl?"

Kinsey gulped. Covered in flour, caught in Becket's arms…

This wasn't how she pictured her reunion with the Grayson clan.

Chapter 4

Becket ran a hand through his hair, and a puff of white dust flew out in a cloud around him. "No fire, but an issue you should all be aware of."

"We're listening," Nash said.

Turning to Kinsey, Becket took her arm and drew her forward. "You remember Kinsey Philips?"

"Sure, we remember Kinsey." Nash glanced at Becket, his brows wrinkling. "She was in my high school graduating class."

"Yeah, she used to ride horses with us." Rider's eyes narrowed. "Is that you, Kinsey?"

Kinsey scrubbed the flour from her face, her checks red beneath. "Yeah. It's me. I was just...um...making chicken and dumplings."

"Did you have a fight with the chicken?" Chance chuckled. "I think the chicken won."

Lily stepped past Becket and Kinsey, sniffing. "Is that what smells so good?"

"We were making the dumplings and got a little carried away." Becket brushed at the front of his shirt.

"I'd say." Nash glanced around at the flour all over the kitchen. "Mom would have a fit."

"We'll clean it up," Kinsey said.

"The point is…" Becket rested a hand on Kinsey's shoulder. "Kinsey is staying here for a while."

"That's great." Lily grinned. "It'll be nice not being the only female in the house."

"So, why did you call me in?" Rider frowned. "I don't care if she uses my old room."

Kinsey nudged Becket. "Tell them."

Becket nodded. "Kinsey left her ex-boyfriend and expects he might come after her."

Nash's brows dipped. "Left your ex-boyfriend?"

"Yeah. The man abused her." Becket's lips thinned into a straight line. "She thinks he'll try to take her back to Dallas."

Rider braced both hands on his hips.

"Like hell he will."

"Over my dead body," Lily agreed.

"He'll have to go through us to get to her," Chance added.

Becket relaxed a little. "That's what I thought. I don't know what the man is capable of, but he's made a habit of using Kinsey as a punching bag."

"Have you notified the police?" Nash asked.

Becket filled them in on their trip to the attorney, and the clinic. "Kinsey wanted to disappear, but we've convinced her to press charges. A female police officer met with her and the doctor at the clinic. She'll file the complaint."

"I want it on Dillon's record. Maybe by doing so, I'm helping to keep him from hurting another woman."

Nash shook his head. "Once a wife beater…Damn, Kinsey. I'm sorry this happened to you."

"Yeah," Rider agreed. "We all are."

Lily slipped an arm around Kinsey. "And we'll do whatever necessary to keep you safe from that bastard."

"Thanks." Tears filled Kinsey's eyes.

"I didn't want to cause you trouble. I just didn't have anywhere else to go."

"You're no trouble." Nash hugged her. "You're family."

"That's right." Rider walked over to the stove, stirred the pot, and lifted a wooden spoon to his nose. "And I might have to come out to the ranch more often if you're cooking."

Relieved by his family's reaction to Kinsey's dilemma, Becket waved his hands, herding them toward the door. "Let Kinsey and me clean the mess and finish making the dumplings. We'll call you for dinner when it's ready. We can all discuss what to be on the lookout for."

Lily's mouth quirked on the corners. "As long as you're not fighting chickens. We might have to referee."

Tossing her a glare, Becket pointed to the door. "Get out."

His siblings chuckled as they left the kitchen.

When Becket turned to Kinsey, he found her chewing on her bottom lip. "What? I told you they'd be on board with looking out for you."

Kinsey's eyes filled again. "I don't want any of them hurt in the process. Dillon's a big guy, and he's mean."

"And we're not?" Becket puffed out his chest, and then winked. "Come on. Let's clean and cook. We can discuss our plan later."

Over a delicious dinner, the Graysons talked about what they could do to keep Kinsey safe. They all agreed to watch for Dillon if he came to town searching, and to let the authorities know. The restraining order would help legally, but from what Kinsey had told them about Dillon, they figured the man would likely ignore the legal document.

After dishes were cleared, Rider left for his apartment in town, Lily and Chance offered to do the dishes, and Nash made one last pass to check on the livestock. Kinsey excused herself to shower off the flour still clinging to her hair and skin.

Becket wandered outside and stood on the porch, staring at the moon without really seeing it. What had he gotten himself into? No matter what, he'd have taken Kinsey in. No one should have to endure what she'd been through. She deserved a better life.

At the same time, he wished for somewhere else she could go. The flour fight in the kitchen had nearly ended in an action he couldn't have taken back. Her face all covered in flour, her green eyes sparkling, and her lips...so damned kissable.

Despite what she'd suffered at Dillon's hand, Kinsey was still recovering from a bad situation. She needed time to recuperate, to get over all the trauma of having a man hitting her.

He dropped into one of the matching rocking chairs he and his siblings had given to his parents for their thirty-fifth anniversary. For a man who made decisions and acted on them immediately, he disliked waiting. And the fact he had no control over the situation was doubly frustrating. The legal system had to run its course. Hopefully by the next day, Dillon would be served the restraining order.

Becket also knew a legal document didn't stop some men. If Massey would break the law by assaulting Kinsey, he'd have no compunction about violating a restraining order. The Graysons had to keep Kinsey safe.

The door opened, and a petite figure stepped out on the porch, barefoot, wearing an oversized T-shirt and not much else. Kinsey. She sat on the steps and leaned her back against the column, legs stretched out in front of her, the moonlight glancing off them.

Becket's pulse jumped and his groin tightened. He could imagine those legs wrapped around his waist as he thrust—

Holy hell, where was he going with that thought? Not anywhere he should be. For a long time, Becket sat still, drinking in Kinsey's silhouette, studying the curve of her ankles, her knees, the way her hair fell down her back in soft waves.

Kinsey drew her legs close, wrapped her arms around them, and rested her chin on her knees. Her shoulders shook.

If Becket wasn't mistaken, he heard a sniffle. His chest clenched, and he listened harder.

Her sniffle was followed by another.

Kinsey reached up and wiped her hand across her cheek.

Becket rose from the rocker and crossed to where she sat.

Kinsey gasped and twisted around. "Oh, Becket. I didn't see you." She started to rise. "I'll go back inside."

"No." He touched a hand to her shoulder. "Please stay." He dropped down beside her.

She laughed, the sound catching on a sob. "I'm sorry. I just can't stop. I haven't cried this much since my parents died."

"Maybe it's time you did." He slipped an arm around her.

Kinsey leaned into him. "I refused to cry when Dillon hit me. Showing weakness seemed to give him more power over me."

Becket's arm tightened around her back. "He's a bastard and a coward. Any man who hits a woman is lower than snake spit."

Her body stiffened against him. Then her shoulders trembled and shook.

At first, Becket thought she was sobbing again. Then he heard her chuckle.

"Snake spit?" The laughter bubbled up and caught on a hiccup. "Is there such a thing?" She looked up at him, moonlight glinting off her watery eyes.

He couldn't get past the eyes and lips to form a functional thought or sentence. "What?"

Kinsey slid her tongue across her bottom lip, her gaze dropping to Becket's mouth. "What?"

Becket swallowed a groan and fought to keep from closing the few short inches between them to steal a kiss.

Just one kiss.

Kinsey's fingers curled into his shirt, and then flattened on his chest. With a jerk, she pushed to her feet. "I'm sorry. I'm taking advantage of your kindness. I've already been a burden and stolen way too much of your time."

Becket rose and grabbed her hand. "You're no burden, and you can't steal what I give freely." He pulled her back into his arms. "I wish this wasn't happening to you, but I'm glad you came here."

She touched his chest, but didn't look up into his eyes. "Thank you."

The sound of a telephone ringing disturbed the quiet of the night.

"I'd better go to bed, if I plan on

helping with the morning chores." She turned and entered the house.

Chance stood in the hallway, the cordless phone pressed to his ear.

Kinsey passed him and climbed the stairs.

Becket started to follow, but Chance snagged his arm. "Wait. There's a fire at the Double Diamond Ranch."

Becket's attention switched to his brother and the conversation on the phone.

When Chance hung up, he sighed. "I just got off duty, but they're calling for all volunteers to head that way."

"What kind of fire?"

"Barn fire."

"Damn. The Double Diamond has at least thirty thoroughbreds. I hope they got them out."

"It's a big barn," Chance said, with a shake of his head. "With conditions as dry as they are, the house and other outbuildings are at risk."

"Are you going?" Becket asked.

"Yeah. If I'm not needed, I'll come home. Better to throw too many people at it than not enough. The pump truck and engine have been dispatched and should be there in the next ten minutes."

"On it." Becket took the stairs two at a time.

Kinsey stood at the top of the landing, a frown marring her brow. "What's wrong?"

Becket didn't slow, calling out as he passed, "Fire at the Double Diamond."

"Is there anything I can do?" She followed him to the door of his room.

He yanked off his good shirt, and then pulled an old T-shirt over his head. "We can always use someone to staff the relief station and hand out drinking water." He paused and raised his brows. "Unless you want to see me in my underwear, I suggest you go put on some clothes. You can ride along."

Kinsey spun and darted out of his doorway.

By the time Becket had changed into old jeans and pulled on his cowboy boots, he spotted Kinsey waiting in the hallway, wearing a pair of jeans from the thrift store.

Though in a hurry, Becket couldn't help but notice how much better they hugged her curves.

She was hopping on one foot, pulling on a red cowboy boot. When she straightened, she tucked the big T-shirt into the waistband of her jeans. "Ready."

Becket ran down the stairs, Kinsey behind him.

Nash and Chance were on the back porch, gathering personal protective equipment from hooks on the wall—fire resistant jackets, pants, boots, and helmets. They headed for Nash's truck, climbed in, and sped away.

Becket grabbed his gear and tossed Kinsey the helmet with a wink. "Make yourself useful."

She caught the helmet and ran to keep up with him. "Yes, sir."

"Hey, wait for me." Lily ran out the back door, wearing old jeans and a faded shirt. She grabbed the last set of gear and hurried to climb in the back seat of Becket's truck.

"How long have you all been volunteer firefighters?"

"I joined the club after I finished college." Becket tipped his head to the rear.

"Lily joined last year. She's still a rookie."

"Hey. I've been on several fires now."

Becket winked. "She's still a rookie."

Lily whacked the back of his head with her palm. "And you're a pain in the ass."

The rest of the ride to the Double Diamond was completed in relative silence. Until Becket saw the fire, he didn't know what to expect. It might already be out by the time he got there.

As he pulled through the gates of the Double Diamond, he got his answer. The bright orange flame rising into the indigo night was the first clue the fire wasn't out, and it might take a little longer to get the blaze under control.

Becket wondered if he'd brought Kinsey into a danger she was ill prepared to handle.

Kinsey sat silent in the seat beside Becket, one hand clutching the door handle. As they neared the ranch house and barn, she tipped her head, following the flames into the night sky where embers spewed like so many fireworks.

Her heart beat faster as the truck pulled to a halt beside others. Dark figures moved close to the fire, stretching a hose from a fire engine to a huge box-like pool being unfolded and filled with the water from a tanker truck.

Becket turned to Kinsey. "Stay back with the other support staff. Don't get near the firemen, or the fire. You don't want to get run over or burned." He reached behind the seat and unearthed a baseball cap. "Cover your hair, you don't want an ember to set it on fire."

"Will do." She stuffed her hair into the cap.

Becket dropped out of the truck, pulled on his protective gear and helmet, and then loped toward the others.

Kinsey eased to the ground and walked toward a group of women standing back from the fire. A table had been set up, and folding chairs were lined up around it. A huge insulated jug sat on the table with disposable cups. Glancing back at the action, Kinsey lost track of which man was Becket. They all looked similar, dressed in the heavy, fire-retardant trousers and jackets.

When the box-shaped pool was full, the tanker drove out of the barnyard and back down the road leading off the ranch. The man who'd unrolled the hose dropped it into the water, waved and shouted to the others manning the fire engine.

Other firefighters held onto a hose leading from the engine to the barn. As soon as the man at the engine turned on the pump, the hose inflated, and water spewed out onto the fire.

"Are you with one of the Graysons?" an older woman asked. She wore a cowboy hat, jeans, and a long-sleeved shirt.

"I am." Kinsey held out a hand. "Kinsey Phillips."

The older woman shook the proffered hand. "Brenda Welsh." Mouth pinched in a tight line, she nodded toward the burning building. "That's our barn."

"I'm so sorry." Kinsey glanced around at everything visible in the light from the raging fire. "Is there anything I can do to help?"

"You can help with the drinks. When the men get too hot, they switch out. It'll be a while before they come our way. In the meantime, if you see an ember burning on the ground, stomp it out, or soak one of these burlap sacks in water from this trough and beat it out." She handed Kinsey a burlap sack and gave her a twisted smile. "Nothing like disaster to bring a community together, right?"

Kinsey grabbed one of the burlap sacks and soaked it in the water from a horse trough. Then the wind shifted toward them. Burning embers fell from the sky, landing on the dry grass and starting spot fires. Kinsey raced around the yard, batting at the mini-fires with the wet burlap sack or stomping them out with her boots. The wind shifted again, and Kinsey walked back to the table with the water jug, sweating, but satisfied she'd helped for the moment.

"Phillips." Brenda glanced toward the sky, her brow puckering. "I knew some Phillips."

Kinsey waited.

"Linda and Randy Phillips. They owned a little place near the Graysons.

Good people." She looked at Kinsey. "They had one child. A daughter. That you?"

Kinsey's heart warmed. In Dallas, no one knew anyone unless they met at work or in church. The big city was impersonal and cold. In rural areas, the neighbors might be a mile apart, but they knew each other. She nodded. "Linda and Randy were my parents."

"It was a sad day when they died. I wondered what happened to their daughter." She smiled at Kinsey. "Look at you, all grown up. I don't recall seeing you since you were in high school." The woman hugged her.

The warm gesture was so surprising that tears sprung to Kinsey's eyes.

Within minutes, Brenda introduced Kinsey to four other women, there as support to the men, or gearing up to pitch in and fight the fire.

So much for keeping her existence a secret in Hellfire. But Kinsey didn't care. These people were friendly and caring, making her feel part of the community.

A loud crack sounded, and the fire leaped higher. Sparks and burning embers shot out from the top of the barn.

"Stand back!" Someone shouted. "The roof's going!"

The men closest to the building scrambled backward, dragging the huge hose with them.

One man tripped and went down at the same time as the roof caved in, pushing the flame-engulfed walls sideways. Burning lumber crashed down on top of the firefighter, trapping him beneath.

Men shouted and ran toward the flames.

On reflex, Kinsey took several steps in that direction when a hand reached out and snagged her arm.

"Kinsey, don't." Brenda stood beside her. "They have the training and know what they're doing. You'd only be in the way and possibly cause more injuries."

Brenda was right. But standing back and watching was almost more than Kinsey could bear. What if the man beneath the rubble was Becket? Or if he was one of the firefighters racing into the blaze to save the trapped man. They could be burned severely, or suffer from smoke inhalation.

Or die.

The men holding the hose trained the water on the wall of boards covering the downed man, extinguishing the flames. Men nearest raced in and lifted the still-smoldering boards while others dragged the injured firefighter from beneath.

Kinsey let go of the breath she'd been holding. But the danger wasn't over. The fire still raged in the barn, and the man who'd been trapped wasn't moving.

Paramedics took over. They removed the man's helmet, checked for a pulse, slipped an oxygen mask over his face, and rolled him onto a backboard. Once secured, they lifted him into the waiting ambulance and drove out of the barnyard.

"Who was it?" Kinsey whispered, her knuckles pressed against her mouth.

"Here come some of the crew," Brenda said. "They'll let us know."

A tall, broad-shouldered man tromped toward them, his face and suit covered in soot. Kinsey could tell it was Becket by the way he swaggered. She ran forward and threw her arms around him. "Becket. Oh, thank God."

He caught her in his arms. "Hey, hey," he chuckled. "I'm okay, but I could use a drink."

Kinsey spun and filled one of the cups. "Who was injured?"

Becket accepted the water and swallowed it quickly. "John LaRue."

Her heart pinched. "Little Johnny? The boy who chased me around the playground when I was in grade school?"

Handing her the cup, Becket winked. "He's twenty-four, and a damned good firefighter now. I have to get back." He cupped her cheek and stared into her eyes.

For a moment, Kinsey thought he might kiss her. She leaned toward him, but she caught herself before her mouth met his. Shock made her take a step backward. "Be careful."

Becket turned and walked back to the inferno, his form silhouetted against the orange and yellow flames.

Kinsey pressed her fingers to her lips. Hell, she'd caused him enough trouble already, she didn't have to add starry-eyed groupie to the list. She had no business kissing or flirting with any of the Grayson men. They'd all been good enough to give her a place to stay. The very least she could do was to stay out of Becket's way and, for her own sake, refrain from kissing him.

Chapter 5

Two hours later, nothing much was left of the barn but a pile of ashes and smoldering timbers. Due to the firefighters' persistence, the house remained unscathed, and the Welsh family still had a home to sleep in, for what was left of the night.

Tired and thankful no one else was hurt, Becket stripped out of his protective gear and tossed it into the back of his truck. He still reeked of smoke, but he felt a thousand pounds lighter.

Chance, Rider, Nash, and Lily looked all done in, their shoulders drooping.

Lily waved to Becket. "I'll ride back with Chance."

Which left Becket alone with Kinsey in his truck. He was finding that alone with Kinsey was not a good thing. The more he was around her, the more he wanted to hold her, touch her, and kiss her pretty pink lips.

He found himself hoping she was well and truly over Massey, so Becket could have a chance with her. How long did women take to get over a bad relationship? He wasn't sure he could put off kissing her for much longer.

Kinsey joined him at the truck after helping Mrs. Welsh and the other ladies put away the jug of water, cups, and the folding table. Knowing she was there had filled him with a bigger sense of purpose and comfort. Whenever he looked back at the ladies gathered around the table, he knew she was safe. If he'd left her behind at the ranch house, he'd have worried, thus taking his attention away from a dangerous situation.

Becket wasn't certain how soon Dillon would be served with the restraining order. From Kinsey's accounting of her past experiences, the man wouldn't let her go easily. "Sorry, I smell pretty bad. Maybe you should drive while I ride in the back."

She laughed. "I think we all smell smoky. It's nothing a shower and laundry won't cure." Kinsey climbed into the truck.

Becket slid into the driver's seat, started the engine, and drove off the Double Diamond Ranch.

"How did you join the volunteer

firefighting group?" Kinsey asked.

"I told them I wanted in." Becket shot her a glance. "Why?"

"If I stay in this area, I want in." She smiled in his direction. "Nothing was more frustrating than to stand back and do nothing."

"Yeah, but you're so…small."

She straightened her shoulders. "I might be small, but I'm stronger than you think."

The thought of Kinsey carrying a heavy hose or charging into a burning building made Becket's stomach clench. "It's not easy. The PPE, personal protective equipment, we wear is heavy, even without the oxygen tanks. On top of that, the pressure from a water hose is enough to knock men as big as I am flat on my ass."

"Lily is a volunteer, isn't she?" Kinsey pointed out.

"Yes."

"Surely, there's something I could do. And I'd like to be included in the training. Every man and woman who lives in a rural community needs to know how to defend their lives, loved ones, and property from fires, don't they?"

He nodded, a smile curling his lips. "You're right. I shouldn't judge the small size of the package. My father always says: where there's a will, there's a way."

"I have the will." Her head jerked in a quick nod.

He liked her spunk. And to think, her ex wanted to beat it out of her. Becket's hands tightened on the steering wheel. What he wouldn't give to pound the bastard into the ground.

At the house, he climbed down and came around to help Kinsey out of the truck, exhaustion making his steps slower. He set her on the ground and, before he could think about what he was doing, he brushed a light kiss across her forehead. "Thank you for helping. You didn't have to come, but I'm glad you did."

"I couldn't have stayed behind, wondering what was happening," she said, her face turned up to his. She touched her hand to his chest. "I almost had kittens when I saw that wall fall on John LaRue. For a minute, I thought *you* were the one trapped."

Becket took her hand and touched his lips to her fingertips. "Thanks for worrying about me."

She stared up into his eyes, heart thumping against her ribs. Then she rose on her tiptoes and pressed her lips to his.

The kiss may have been a soft brush of her mouth against his, but it was the spark that ignited the flame.

Becket's arms circled Kinsey's waist and he crushed her to him, his lips coming down on hers, claiming her mouth. She gasped, her mouth opening enough for his tongue to slide inside, to twist with hers, caressing the length. He tasted smoke and a hint of minty toothpaste.

She sighed and laced her fingers around the back of his neck, dragging him closer.

What started as a simple *thank you,* exploded into something hotter, more combustible and all-consuming. The sound of a squeaky door hinge made Becket back away. He dropped his arms to his sides and stared down at her, his chest heaving.

Kinsey raised her fingers to her lips, her eyes round, her erratic breathing making her chest rise and fall rapidly.

"Becket? You out there?" Lily called from the back porch.

Thankfully, the truck blocked her view of him doing something he should never have done. "I'm here," he responded, stepping into view. "What do you need?"

"Could you make sure the chickens are locked in the coop? I thought I saw something moving around when we came in. If it's a coyote, I don't want it to get to the laying hens."

He lifted a hand in a casual wave. "Will do."

"Thanks." Lily reentered the house and closed the door.

"Do you need help checking on the chickens?" Kinsey asked.

Her voice was low, gravelly, and so sexy, Becket's groin tightened. "No," he said, firming his resolve. "You should go inside."

Before I kiss you again.

She started to turn away, paused, and touched his arm. "That shouldn't have happened."

"Hell, yeah. But I'm not sorry it

did." He brushed a strand of her hair back behind her ear. "I can't take it back."

"Nor can I." Her chest rose and fell on a sigh. "But I can't let it happen again."

"Okay." Though he wanted to pull her back into his embrace, he restrained himself. "You'd better take a number for the shower. I'll be in shortly."

He spun on his heels and headed for the barn and chicken house. Resistance wasn't working for him. Which meant the farther away from Kinsey, the better.

Grabbing a flashlight, they kept hung on the inside of the barn, Becket made a perfunctory inspection of the chicken house and yard. No sign of coyotes. He shined a beam at the ground. The only prints in the dust were human. No animal tracks. As Becket made a turn around the exterior of the barn, he had the odd feeling of being watched. Shining the flashlight beam outward, he panned the surrounding corral, pasture, and outbuildings. Nothing moved, yet the shadows took on a more sinister feel.

Becket shrugged, writing it off as exhaustion.

Tomorrow, he hoped to hear news from Natalie about the restraining order. He almost hoped Dillon would make a play for Kinsey. Becket would love a chance to show the man what being battered and thrown around like a rag doll felt like. He'd give the son of a bitch a taste of what he'd done to Kinsey.

Kinsey tossed and turned through the night, waking with a headache and tightness in her chest. She suspected the headache was from lack of adequate sleep and inhaling too much smoke the night before. The source of the tightness in her chest had to be what kept her from sleeping. Her girlhood crush on Becket had exploded into a full-blown ache that couldn't be satisfied with a single kiss. Though the kiss had been hot. Really hot.

Leaving her bed just after dawn, Kinsey dressed in the freshly laundered clothes she'd picked out at the thrift shop, brushed her teeth and hair, and headed for the kitchen. At the very least, she could make herself useful. By the time the Graysons entered the kitchen, she had coffee brewing, bacon, toast, and scrambled eggs cooked.

A yawning Lily made a beeline for the coffee. "Smells good enough to drink."

"What are you talking about?" Chance entered behind her, crossed to the stove, and snagged a piece of bacon. "It smells good enough to eat." He took a bite and moaned. "Heaven. Pure heaven."

"We need to keep Kinsey around." Nash filled a plate with fluffy yellow scrambled eggs, bacon, and toast and sat at the table.

Kinsey's insides warmed. After living in a house where she'd been made to feel like the inferior being, she liked being surrounded by people who appreciated her efforts.

Lily and Chance filled their plates, claimed seats around the table, and dug into the food.

Then Becket stepped into the kitchen, and Kinsey's pulse quickened and heat rose into her cheeks. She turned away and filled a plate for him.

"Aren't you eating breakfast?" Lily asked.

With Becket's plate in her hand, Kinsey turned from the stove.

The cowboy stood at the back door. "Nah. I'm not hungry. I've got animals to feed and a fence needing mending in the south pasture."

"If you can wait, I can help when I get off work this afternoon," Chance offered.

"I don't go on duty until five o'clock this afternoon, I can give you a hand this morning," Nash said. "Just let me finish my breakfast."

Becket shook his head. "No need, it's a one-man job."

"I'm working in town today," Lily announced. "Some of the elementary school staff are conducting a Learning is Fun Day at the library. We're expecting at least two-dozen kids. Otherwise, I'd help. I don't know when I'll be back. Don't wait dinner on me."

Without responding, Becket left the house.

Somewhat deflated, Kinsey set the plate of food in the middle of the table. "Y'all eat up."

"Aren't you eating?" Lily asked, a frown wrinkling her brow.

"I already did," Kinsey lied. Her appetite had gone out the door with Becket. She cleaned the pan she'd used, wiped the counters, and left the rest of the Graysons in the kitchen.

Kinsey hurried up the stairs to Rider's old room and pulled on her cowboy boots, disappointed with the complete brush-off Becket had given her. She'd already decided keeping her distance was the best course of action, but did he have to be so cold and withdrawn? He'd barely glanced her way. At first she was angry, but as she descended the stairs, she had to admit, he was right. Beyond a doubt, her previous relationship was over, but she wasn't ready for a new one.

By the time Kinsey reentered the kitchen, she saw the other Graysons had dispersed. From the quiet in the house, they'd either left or gone outside. That gave her the privacy she needed to call Natalie and check the status of the restraining order.

Natalie answered on the third ring.

"Hi, Natalie, it's Kinsey Phillips."

"Hi, Kinsey. I'm glad you called. I have good news and bad news."

Kinsey sucked in a deep breath and dropped into the nearest chair. "Go ahead." A lump of fear lodged in her throat.

"My contacts in Dallas convinced a judge to sign off on the restraining order yesterday. The sheriff attempted to serve Mr. Massey."

"Attempted?" Kinsey's stomach sank to her knees.

"That's the bad news. Mr. Massey wasn't home. When the sheriff went to the Cowboys' practice field, he verified everyone was there but Dillon."

Her heart kicked up the pace, and she felt lightheaded. "Not there?"

"No one has seen him since the day before yesterday." Natalie paused. "I'm worried about you, Kinsey."

"I'm okay."

"Yeah, until Massey finds you. Be sure you're with one of the Graysons at all times. Hopefully, Massey won't try anything with others around."

With her pulse pounding so loud she

barely heard Natalie, she thanked her and hung up.

Needing the reassuring presence of a friendly face, Kinsey left the house and went in search of Becket. She found him working on a water trough in one of the pastures. She climbed over the wooden rail fence and dropped to the ground. "Need help?"

"No. I'm almost done here, and then I'm headed out to mend the fence I mentioned." He straightened and wiped his hands on his jeans. Water poured into the trough. "That should do it."

"What was wrong with it?"

"The horses must have bumped the float. It was reading full all the time, so the valve wouldn't release to refill the tank." He turned and studied her face. "What's wrong?"

"Nothing," she answered, too quickly. He must have seen the strain in her face, because he pulled her into his arms.

"You talk to Natalie?"

A lump formed in her throat. "Yeah."

"And?"

"They couldn't serve Dillon with the restraining order, because they can't find him. He hasn't been to practice in two days." She curled her fingers into Becket's shirt. "He'll find me."

"He might find you, but he won't hurt you, if I have a say in it." Becket's arms tightened around her reassuringly.

She let his warmth seep into her. *Just for another moment.* She wanted to soak in the security his presence provided.

He held her for a long time, then tilted her chin up and stared into her eyes. "You'll be okay."

She nodded. "If you say so."

"You need to believe that. Until you do, you'll always be looking over your shoulder."

"Wouldn't you? I'm not a big guy, like you." She stepped back. "Dillon weighs twice as much as I do. He could snap me in two like that." Kinsey snapped her fingers.

"Then stay with me. Between the two of us, we'll keep you safe." He kissed her forehead. "Okay?"

Better than okay.

She wanted to tip up her head to

capture his lips. But she'd been the one to tell him not to kiss her again. With her life as messed up as it was, she had no business kissing Becket. He deserved better. Stepping back, she forced a smile. "What can I help with?"

"I have the four-wheeler loaded up with supplies. If you'll go get it from the barn, then we can head out to fix that fence."

She popped a mock salute, performed an about face, and hurried off to the barn, praying she still knew how to drive an ATV. Kinsey found it parked a few feet inside the open door of the barn. As she slung her leg over the seat, she glanced around. A prickling feeling crawled over the back of her neck. Nothing stirred in the barn. The stalls were empty, the horses turned out to graze in the pasture. Not even a barn cat came out to greet her. Still, Kinsey felt as if someone was watching her.

Shaking it off as an overactive imagination, she turned the key and pressed the starter switch. The ATV roared to life. Kinsey released the brake, pressed her thumb on the throttle lever, and the four-wheeler leaped forward. Tools rattled in the large metal box attached to the back.

By the time she reached Becket, she had the vehicle figured out. She pulled to a stop beside him, letting the engine idle, and started to climb off.

"Stay." Becket waved at her. "I'll ride behind you."

Her belly clenched and her core heated. "Is there another one of these in the barn?"

"The other one isn't working right now. Either we take this and ride double, or we drive the truck." He glanced at the sunny sky. "Personally, I was looking forward to the wind in my hair. You can drive."

She couldn't argue with that, and gave up pretending to want to ride separately. As Becket mounted behind her and his long, muscular legs wrapped around hers, Kinsey could barely put together a functional thought. "Which way?" Her voice came out in a strained squeak.

He pointed. "South."

She gunned the throttle, and the little four-wheeler shot off across the pasture.

The wind blew through her hair, giving her a sense of freedom she hadn't felt since she'd left Hellfire to go to college. The incredibly sexy man on the vehicle behind her only fueled her excitement, making it burn like a wildfire. By the time they reached the damaged portion of the fence, she was laughing out loud and smiling so wide, she was sure to catch a bug in her teeth. But she didn't care.

She approached the fence a little faster than she should have and whipped the handlebar to the right, skidding sideways to a halt. "Wow!" Kinsey switched off the motor, her hands still vibrating to the rhythm of the small engine. "I'd forgotten how much fun these are."

Becket dismounted, brushed the dust off his jeans, and resettled his cowboy hat on his head. "I believe I saw my life pass before my eyes."

Kinsey backhanded him in the belly. "Oh, don't be a baby. You used to drive that fast when you were a teen. I remember. Nash and I never could keep up with you."

He captured her hand and pulled her

against his chest. "In case you haven't noticed, we're not teens anymore."

Adrenaline powering through her veins already meant being that close to Becket only made her heart pump faster. "N-no, we're not." She looked up into his eyes.

The intensity of his blue gaze made her shiver with desire in the hot Texas sun.

Becket swallowed hard, his grip tightening on hers. "Let's fix a fence." He released her and stepped away.

Kinsey willed herself to relax. Nothing would happen between the two of them. She wasn't ready mentally, even if her body was screaming for action.

Moments later, Becket had a strand of new barbed wire nailed to a post. Holding the roll of wire on a stick, he walked fifty feet down the fence-line and settled it on the ground.

Kinsey followed on the four-wheeler, jostling over the uneven ground. Already, her injuries didn't hurt as badly as they had the day before.

Becket tied the barbed wire to the back of the four-wheeler. "You're driving.

But this time, ease forward slowly."

She knew the drill. Stretching fence wire involved a fine line between tightening the wire gently, and pulling too hard and breaking it. With her hand on the brake, she barely touched her other hand on the throttle lever. The ATV rolled forward.

"More," Becket called out over the roar of the engine.

She eased forward a few more inches.

"Stop."

Kinsey pressed the brake and held it.

Using solid strokes, Becket nailed the wire into the fence post. "Okay, back it up a little to ease the tension."

Kinsey did as instructed.

Becket cut the wire, bent it over, and nailed it again. With the wire in place, the fence was as good as new.

A sense of pride washed over Kinsey. She hadn't worked on a ranch since she'd lived next door. She missed the outdoors and the sense of accomplishment in doing something physical. Switching off the ATV, she climbed down and admired Becket's handiwork. "You're pretty good at that."

He shrugged and loaded his tools into the toolbox on the back of the ATV. "I've mended a few fences."

She jerked a thumb over her shoulder. "What do you suppose broke this one?"

"That bull." He pointed out in the pasture. "He's huge, he's ornery, and he's a staunch believer in 'the grass is always greener on the other side of the fence'."

Kinsey turned to see a huge black bull running toward them. "Uh, should we be concerned? Will he stop?" She backed up, bumping into Becket.

His arms came around her. "Sometimes he does. Doesn't look like he's going to, this time."

"Becket?" Kinsey turned and buried her face in his shirt. "Let's get out of here."

His arms tightened. "I think it's too late."

The thunder of heavy hooves against hard-packed earth filled Kinsey's ears. She glanced back at the bull, then grabbed Becket's hand, and tugged hard. "He's going to kill us. Move!"

Becket stood still. "Get behind me."

"What good will that do? If he hits you, he'll take out both of us." Kinsey's heart hammered against her ribs. "We need to climb over the fence. Now!"

The more frantic she became, the calmer Becket appeared. He stuck his hand into his jeans pocket as if he hadn't a care in the world.

The bull charged forward.

Becket pushed her behind him, where she clung to his back, trying desperately to pull him aside. A bull weighing close to two tons could kill a man.

"Please, Becket. Don't let him hurt you," she whispered, her heart leaping to her throat.

The bull was almost upon them when it skidded to a halt, a cloud of dust rising at his feet.

Then, as pretty as you please, Becket held out three lumps of sugar in his palm.

With a sniff, the bull reached out with his fat bovine lips and gobbled up the sugar cubes. Then he nuzzled Becket's jeans, looking for more.

"Go on, you big mooch." Becket

shoved at the bull's head.

With no more sugar to be had, the bull wandered off.

Kinsey rounded on Becket, glaring. "You could have told me you had a pet bull, instead of letting me believe we were going to die."

"And miss the drama?" He chuckled. "You should have seen your face."

"What? The look of stark terror?"

"Well, yeah." His chuckle returned. "You have to agree, it's funny now. Boris is nothing but a big teddy bear with a love of sugar." He pulled her into his embrace. "Besides, saving you from Boris gave me a chance to prove I can protect you against man or beast."

"I'm beginning to believe *you're* the beast." She smacked his chest softly. "I really thought that bull would kill us." Her lips twitched, and laughter bubbled up her throat. "Then he stopped and ate the sugar…" She shook her head and laughed. "Yeah, I wasn't expecting that. And you, the hero, ready to stop the freight train by putting out your hand." She narrowed her eyes. "You're no hero, Becket Grayson."

Something big leaned into her, shoving her forward into Becket's arms.

He pulled her close and turned to the bull, which nuzzled his hand for more sugar. "No more. Go on." Becket slapped the bull's hindquarters, and he lumbered off, headed across a big field toward a crowd of cows watching him with interest.

"Are you okay?" Becket asked. He didn't release her.

"Uh, you can let go of me now."

"Do you want me to?" Becket's hands smoothed down her back, applying little pressure.

If she really wanted to get away from him, she could. She shook her head, not willing to put into words what her body was feeling.

He tipped her chin. "I'm sorry Boris scared you."

She wanted to stay mad at him, but the image of the big bull licking a sugar cube out of Becket's palm made her want to laugh. Kinsey shook her head, a smile pulling at her lips. "I owe you one."

"No, I owe you an apology." He

pressed a kiss to her forehead. "I'm sorry."

"Really? That's the best you can do?" she whispered, her arms slipping up around his neck. "You made me think we were going to die."

"You're right. I'm really..." He pressed a kiss to her eyelid, "...really," another kiss to her cheek, "...really," now to the tip of her nose.

Blood pounding in her veins, Kinsey caught his face between her palms. "You're getting warmer, but you're taking too long." She leaned up on her toes, pulling him down at the same time. "Just do it."

Chapter 6

If she'd told him to let go, he would have. In a heartbeat. But she didn't. When his lips touched hers, there was no going back. He claimed her mouth, tracing the seam with his tongue until she opened to him and met him halfway. Becket slid his hands down her back, cupped her ass, and lifted her.

She wrapped her legs around his waist and her arms around his neck, deepening the kiss.

In the middle of a Texas field, the hot sun beating down on him, Becket had never felt heat as intense as what was inside him.

Kinsey was incredible. Her body fit perfectly against his, her curves soft and sexy. He carried her to the four-wheeler and set her on her feet, releasing his hold.

Mouth open, she stared at him, her chest rapidly rising and falling.

Becket slid his hand around her waist and up beneath her shirt, loving the feel of her skin against his fingertips, but careful not to press on the bruises her ex-boyfriend had given her.

She closed her eyes and inhaled deeply.

He hesitated.

Then her hands rose to cup his, guiding them upward to the swells of her breasts.

His groin tightened, his jeans suddenly too snug.

Once she had him where she wanted him, she released his hand and lowered hers to the hem of her shirt. Slowly, she raised it up her torso and over her head, revealing full breasts encased in a white lacy bra.

"Are you sure?" he asked. "You've been through a lot."

Her brows dipped. "Do you have protection?"

He slipped one hand into his back pocket and handed her his wallet.

She flipped it open and found a foil packet. A slow smile spread across her lips. "I remember. You were a Boy Scout."

He pocketed his wallet. "Always prepared."

Holding his gaze, she tucked the packet into his front pocket, shifted her fingers to the button on his jeans, and flicked it open.

Becket sucked in a sharp breath when she pulled his T-shirt out of his waistband, her knuckles brushing against his taut abs.

His cock hardened instantly, pushing against the zipper holding him back.

Not for long.

Kinsey slid down the tab slowly, carefully, until his shaft sprang out into her palm. She closed her hand around him, and her tongue slipped out to moisten her pink lips.

Holy hell, she was lighting him on fire.

Becket snagged the front of her jeans, flipped the button through the hole, and yanked down the zipper. Lace panties matching the bra peeked out of the opening. He groaned, slid his hand into the denim, and cupped her sex. "Say the word, and I'll stop." *God only knows how.* But if she wanted to stop, he would.

"Don't you dare," she whispered,

toeing off her boots to stand barefoot in the dry Texas soil. Then she shimmied out of her jeans and kicked them to the side. She stood before him in nothing but her bra and panties, her ivory skin a stark contrast to raven hair falling down around her shoulders in large, loose curls and the purple bruises scattered across her torso.

"Kinsey, you're beautiful."

She cupped his cock in her palm and slid her fingers down to the base. "You're not so bad yourself."

Becket hooked his finger in the elastic of her panties and dragged them down. She stepped out of the silky scrap of material, and he wadded and stuffed them into his pocket. Before he straightened, he pressed a kiss to the tuft of hair over her mons.

"How…" she whispered, her word catching on a gasp.

"Like this." Becket straddled the ATV, his cock sticking out of his jeans, straight and proud. Once he was seated, he scooted back and held out his hand. "Come here."

She took his hand and swung her leg

over his, settling in his lap, facing him. "I've never done it in the open." Kinsey laughed nervously. "Are you sure no one will come up on us?"

"No. But that's what makes doing this more exciting. Almost dangerous."

Her eyes widened and her nostrils flared.

Becket wanted her to be ready when he took her. She'd gone through so much. Even though they were out on the prairie, he could make the loving as good for her as it was for him. He slid his hand between her legs and dipped a finger into her channel. Sweet Jesus, she was so warm and wet.

He nearly came, he was so hot for her. Holding onto his control by a thread, he dipped into her again and dragged his finger up between her folds to that narrow nubbin of flesh. He stroked once.

Kinsey arched her back, her breath caught, and her fingers dug into his shoulders. "Oh, Becket!" she said, her voice ragged and sexy.

He stroked her again, watching the excited expression on her face.

She squeezed her eyes shut and

threw back her head. "Oh, my. Oh, my." Kinsey reached behind her and unclipped her bra, letting it slide off her shoulders. Then she cupped the back of his head and guided him to one of her breasts.

He sucked her into his mouth, greedy to taste her, his tongue swirling around the taut bud, flicking and nibbling. All the while, he strummed her clit until she rocked against him, her body tensing, her fingernails sinking into his shirt. When she went rigid, he knew he had her where he wanted her. He let her ride the wave of her release for several long moments, and then he took the condom from his pocket and rolled it over his cock.

Kinsey pressed her hands against his shoulders and rose.

He gripped her hips and positioned her over him.

"Now," she said, and eased down, taking him inside.

He pulled her hips down, thrusting upward, filling her.

Her channel tightened around him, encasing him like a hot, sweet, wet glove. He could get lost in her. Completely and utterly lost.

Then he was raising and lowering her faster and faster, rocking the little ATV, stirring up dust around them. Within what felt like only moments, sensations inside him built to a powerful crescendo, and he exploded over the top. He thrust one last time, burying himself deep inside her. His arms wrapped around Kinsey, holding her close until they both drifted back to earth.

When he could think and see clearly again, he captured her face in his hands and kissed her, his tongue taking hers in a lingering twist.

A cow mooed in the distance, breaking into their cocoon of silence.

Kinsey leaned back and chuckled softly. "That was my first on a four-wheeler."

"Mine too." He pressed a kiss to one of her nipples and sucked it into his mouth, letting it slide out with a final flick of his tongue. "But I highly recommend it." He became aware of the sun beating down on their bodies. On Kinsey in particular, who was completely naked.

Sweet Jesus, she had a beautiful

body. Now that he could see all of it, the bruises on her breasts, ribs, hips and shoulders stood out against her ivory skin, painful reminders of what her ex had done.

Guilt gnawed at Becket's gut. "I shouldn't have done that. You're not even fully recovered from what that bastard did. Hell, now you probably think all men are animals." He lifted her off him and set her on the ground beside the ATV. He rose, peeled off the condom and zipped his jeans.

Kinsey gathered her clothes, slipping her shirt over her shoulders first, and then dragging her jeans up over her hips. When he saw her nearly topple over pulling on her boots, Becket lifted her onto the ATV and helped her. As soon as they were fully dressed, he captured her face in his hands. "Please don't regret what just happened between us. I don't."

She stared into his eyes, her green gaze suspiciously moist. "I don't. Though, I probably should." With a strangled laugh, she cupped the back of his head and leaned forward to kiss him hard on the mouth. "You can drive back. I don't want to think. I just want to feel the wind in my hair."

Becket drove the four-wheeler back to the ranch house, images of Kinsey's beautiful, bruise-covered body rolling through his mind like a movie track repeating itself again and again. He couldn't let Massey get his hands…or fists…on her ever again. He'd kill the bastard first.

On the return trip, Kinsey rode on the back of the vehicle, her arms wrapped around Becket, her cheek pressed against his back, wondering if she'd just had the best experience of her life, or her worst mistake. After the months of physical and mental abuse, she could fall in love with anyone who was being nice to her after such a horrible situation.

But this was Becket. She'd been in love with him since she could remember. When he'd married while she was in college, she had been heartbroken and turned to Dillon. If anything, he'd been her rebound love. And Dillon had been the biggest mistake of her life.

His jealousy had tainted their relationship almost from the start. Kinsey had been too blind to see it until he'd started hitting.

Becket would never hit a woman. His father had taught him to love and respect women by the example he set with his mother.

As they neared the house, Kinsey almost wanted to tell Becket to turn around and take her away. Maybe they could find a cabin in the woods and live there forever, away from everyone.

Away from Dillon.

Kinsey's gaze scanned the barnyard and the area around the house. By now, Dillon could be in the county. Hell, he could have learned from the ladies who had been at the Double Diamond Ranch that she was staying at the Graysons.

Her heart beat faster, and she shook all over.

Becket pulled the four-wheeler to a stop outside the barn, and she climbed off first. Her knees wobbled beneath her, but she didn't want to show her fear to Becket. She was tired of being a weakling, being afraid of a man who hurt her. She had to stand up for herself. She couldn't let Dillon win. "I'm going to the house for a shower.

Do you want me to fix lunch for you?"

"I'll be up there soon. I want to put things away. We can make lunch together." He smiled and winked. "How do dumplings sound?"

His wink made Kinsey smile. Having Becket around made her feel safe and happy for the first time since her parents died. She leaned up on her toes and kissed him. "I'll wait to start lunch until you come inside." Then she turned and walked up to the house, aware of Becket's gaze on her backside. Or at least, she hoped he was watching. To make it more interesting, she exaggerated the sway of her hips. As she mounted the steps to the back porch, she glanced over her shoulder.

Becket stood beside the ATV, his gaze on her.

She smiled and waved, that happy glow following her inside. Yes. She'd always loved Becket, but she knew she needed to take their new relationship slowly. With emotional scars, she wasn't sure how much of it would carry over. Kinsey didn't want Becket to have to deal with any long-term issues she might have. Still, she wasn't letting anything spoil her good mood.

In the kitchen, she found a note on the table.

Since Kinsey is with you, Lily made a run to town for groceries. Chance went to the diner for lunch, and Nash went to work. Don't do anything we wouldn't. We'll be back later.

Kinsey grinned, glad they didn't know what she and Becket had done out in the south pasture. That act was their secret, one she'd hold dear to her heart. Her core still tingled from the best sex she'd had in a long time.

She climbed the stairs to the second floor, gathered clean clothing, and crossed to the shower, wondering if Becket would hurry back to the house and join her in the shower.

Alas, he might not be aware the ranch was deserted except for the two of them. If he knew, he might be tempted.

She stripped out of the dusty clothes and stared at herself in the mirror. Her body was a colorful mass of bruises. Some purple, others that ugly shade of greenish-yellow. How could a man be attracted to a woman who looked like her?

Another thought made her frown. What if he really was having regrets and was procrastinating out in the barn to avoid facing her?

Kinsey shook herself. Dillon had made her feel unworthy of love. She was free of him, and should free herself of the negative thoughts he'd made her believe.

With purpose in her steps, she entered the shower and turned on the water. Afterward, she'd join Becket in the kitchen. If something happened between them, their relationship was meant to be. If not, perhaps she just needed to be patient. Her life was headed in the right direction. She wasn't going back to the hell she'd lived in before.

After Kinsey disappeared into the house with a sexy smile on her face, Becket revved the ATV engine. The rumble of the machine beneath him seemed to be a metaphor for how he felt at that moment. His divorce three years ago had put him emotionally on hold. No woman was worth the trouble of dating if the relationship would only end up in disappointment, or her leaving him for a richer man.

Until Kinsey. He was attracted to her for who she had been, and who she'd become. However, telling himself over and over to take it slow with her would be futile. He'd never look at his ATV the same. The rumbling engine reminded Becket of Kinsey riding him, with nothing but air covering her skin and blue sky as a backdrop.

She was hot and she was beautiful, her laughing green eyes shining right into his heart. He could fall in love with her, if he let himself. Becket shifted into gear and pressed the throttle.

Take it slowly.

His new mantra repeating in his head, he drove the ATV into the barn and parked it next to the other that needed repair.

Though his body was in the barn, he let his thoughts drift to Kinsey showering in the bathroom across the hall from his bedroom. If he hurried, he could catch her, dripping wet, and in need of someone to dry off her skin. They could move to his bedroom and make love again. This time on the comfortable mattress, taking their time and not risking sunburn on her naked body.

Sweet Jesus. Had he really made love to Kinsey on the seat of the four-wheeler?

Take it slow.

Becket inhaled and let out his breath in a long, slow stream. Kinsey needed to recover before she threw herself into anything. Especially into sex with another man. She had been more than willing, initiating the encounter, but was it the right thing to do? Had he taken advantage of her at a weak moment?

He would give her time. Let her shower as planned, and then meet him in the kitchen to make a sandwich. Not steal a kiss, or take her on the kitchen table. His groin tightened as he struggled to quench his desire.

Feed the horses. Hell, he'd already done that. *Stack some hay.* It was all perfectly stacked, ready to use in the winter. Maybe he could reorganize the tack room. That could kill an hour, if he took his time.

Making his way to the room filled with saddles, bridles, and other equipment, he glanced inside. Well, damn. He'd completely reorganized it a month ago. The equipment was still clean and orderly.

He might as well go to the house and see if Kinsey was done in the shower. Maybe he'd climb the stairs and knock on the door, just to see if she needed anything—fresh towels, toilet paper, someone to pat the moisture off her skin. He groaned and started to turn away from the tack room.

A scuffling sound and a movement out of the corner of his eye caught his attention. Before he could react, something hard hit him in the back of the head.

Pain shot through his skull. Becket staggered into the tack room, his knees buckling.

Fight it. Don't go down.

Another blow to the back of the head sent him crashing to the hardwood floor, and the lights blinked out.

Chapter 7

Kinsey finished a long shower, disappointed Becket hadn't joined her. She'd taken her time drying off, hoping to hear a knock on the bathroom door. In her mind, she already had a plan. She'd drop the towel, plant a hand on his chest, and back him into his bedroom across the hallway.

No knock came to her door. With a sigh, she dressed, dragging her clothing over her sensitized skin, wishing Becket's hands were covering her instead of clothes. She laughed at her imaginings. Kinsey realized having a relationship with someone she trusted was so much better than what she'd had with Dillon.

The house was silent except for the sound of her footsteps as she descended the stairs and entered the kitchen. Becket had obviously stayed to perform needed chores in the barn. Or maybe he regretted making love to her in the pasture.

Deflated and a little sad, Kinsey searched the refrigerator for sandwich ingredients. Deli meat, mustard, mayonnaise, and cheese—everything she needed to make a lunch.

The door creaked open behind her.

"Just in time. I was about to make sandwiches. You can help." She turned with a smile.

"Hello, Kinsey."

All the items slipped from her arms and crashed to the floor as Kinsey faced the man who'd become her living nightmare. "Dillon," she said, her voice barely a whisper, her insides quaking.

Dillon advanced a step. "Imagine how worried I was when I woke up to find you gone."

Kinsey inched backward, her gaze darting around, searching for a way out. All escape routes required passing her exboyfriend. Where was Becket? "I'm sorry. I sh-should have left a note."

He took another step, closing the distance. "You stole my keys out of my pocket."

Stay calm. Her heart slammed against her ribs, pumping so fast her head swam. "I only took the key to *my* car and put the others back."

"You stole them out of my pocket." Another step and he could almost reach her.

Kinsey stepped back and to the side, placing the kitchen island between them. If she remembered correctly, knives were kept in one of the drawers. Which one? She'd only have a single chance to find it.

Dillon's eyes narrowed, and he held out his hand. "You've had your fun, Kinsey. Time to come home."

Kinsey's back stiffened, and her eyes narrowed. "I'm not going back."

"You belong to me."

To me. Not with me. Dillon considered her his property, not his partner. Anger stiffened her muscles. "I don't belong to anyone. Especially not you." Her voice hardened, though her knees shook. She shot a glance toward the open door behind Dillon. Where was Becket?

"Grayson isn't coming to save you." Dillon's lips curled into a sneer. "He's not coming to save anyone ever again."

Her heart stopped, and she clutched the edge of the island. "What do you mean?" Then she smelled smoke coming through the open door, and her pulse leapt. "Dillon, what have you done?"

Dillon's lips peeled back over his teeth in a feral snarl. "Taken away temptation. You're coming home, and you're not ever returning to Hellfire. Now, quit wasting my time. Let's go."

Rage filled her, bubbling over like a boiling cauldron. "Dillon, you're a sick bastard. There is no way in hell I'm going anywhere with you." She yanked open the drawer, grabbed the biggest, sharpest butcher knife she could find, and held it in front of her. "You're never laying a hand on me again."

Dillon gave her his 'public' charming smile and raised his hands as if in surrender.

Something he'd never do. "Baby, I promise. I won't hurt you."

"You forget, I've been with you long enough to know you break all your promises." She circled the island, the knife firmly in her grip. She had no question in her mind that she'd use it if he came at her. Her goal was to get the hell out of the house and find Becket. Her chest tightened as she imagined all the horrible things Dillon could have done to him. And why was smoke drifting through the kitchen door?

"Quit stalling, Kinsey. We're leaving now."

"Then leave. I'm not going with you. Ever. Again."

Dillon lunged for her.

Kinsey jabbed the knife at the hands reaching for her, cutting into his forearm.

He cradled his arm. "You fucking bitch."

Kinsey turned and ran for the door.

Footsteps pounded behind her.

Before she made it through, strong hands grabbed her around the waist and yank her back against him. She slammed the knife into his thigh.

"Bitch, you'll pay for that." With one arm around her middle, Dillon knocked the knife out of her hand with a heavy blow to her wrist.

Pain shot up her arm, but she couldn't give up. Not now. She'd come this far, she couldn't go back. Wouldn't. She jabbed her elbow into his gut and stomped on his instep.

Dillon grunted and wrapped her in a bear hug, trapping her arms to her sides and lifting her off the ground.

Kinsey kicked and twisted, but the more she fought, the tighter he squeezed, until she could barely draw a breath. "Put me down, Dillon. You're breaking the law. I swore out a restraining order against you."

"Yeah, I got the texts from my teammates. How's that working for you?"

Not any better than she'd predicted. The man was insane, and hope began to leach out of her. He was so much bigger, and as strong as an ox. How could a woman of five feet one inch, weighing less than half what he did, fight a man that big?

Use your brain.

Warm, wet blood dripped down her leg. She'd injured him. Based on the strength of his grip, the damage wasn't enough to weaken him. But, the amount of blood on the floor would make it slippery. She let her body go limp, pretending to pass out.

"'bout damn time," Dillon grumbled, loosening his arms slightly.

Kinsey sucked in a deep breath, clearing her head.

Dillon started through the door, but Kinsey jerked her legs up, planted them on the frame, and pushed hard.

He staggered backward, slipping in his own blood. Then, he crashed to the floor, taking Kinsey down.

As soon as he hit the ground, he released her and groaned.

Kinsey was ready. After rolling to the side, she leaped to her feet and scrambled for the exit. The hot Texas sunshine beckoned her, and the fresh air screamed freedom. All she had to do was get there.

Two steps. That's as far as she made it before Dillon swept out his leg. He caught her at the ankles, knocking her feet sideways.

She fell, watching the floor as if it rose up to greet her. Her forehead hit, pain ripped through her, and blackness descended.

Becket coughed, dragged in a breath of hot, acrid smoke, and coughed again. He forced open his eyes and they stung, making them tear. As he fought his way through the fog to consciousness, he took a moment to realize the fog was smoke, and he was awake. Pain throbbed at the back of his head. He pushed to his knees to get a bearing on his location. Stirrups hung in front of his face from saddles perched on saddletrees. Tack room.

His first thought was of the horses. Then he remembered turning them out to pasture earlier.

Becket staggered to his feet, pulled his T-shirt up over his nose, coughing. His eyes burned and smoke filled the air, making seeing in the small room hard. He touched his fingertips to the door and doorknob. They were hot. Which meant the fire was on the other side.

Grabbing a saddle blanket, he wrapped it around the doorknob and twisted. The door didn't budge. He held the knob and threw his shoulder against the wood panel. Still, the door wouldn't open. Something blocked it. He hit the door again with his shoulder. Again, to no avail. If he didn't escape soon, he would be overcome by smoke, or the fire would find its way through the walls, and consume him and everything else in the tack room.

Hunkering low, he felt his way through the cloud of smoke until he found the outside wall. He cleared an old wooden trunk and several saddletrees out of the way, and then kicked at the boards. His first blow did little to budge the nails driven into the beams over fifty years ago when the barn had been built.

Bracing his back against the boards, he cocked his leg and threw everything he had into hitting one board, low to the floor. It moved, the nails sliding out. Kicking again and again, he loosened one board, and then the adjacent one. The smoke thickened, and he couldn't get a clean breath of air. He hacked and coughed, but he didn't give up.

He suspected Dillon Massey had been the man who hit him. The thought of what Dillon might do to Kinsey made Becket kick harder until one board shot free of the brace boards, and Becket could see blue sky. Fresh air seeped in but the smoke prevailed. He worked at another board until it broke. The hole he'd created was barely big enough.

Becket laid flat on the floor of the tack room and squeezed his big body through, sucking in air once his head cleared the barn. With renewed strength, he wiggled, scooted, and crawled inch by inch until he was free of the barn. Coughing, practically hacking up a lung, he staggered to his feet and ran for the house. He didn't know how long he'd been unconscious.

Dillon could be halfway across the county with Kinsey by now.

As Becket reached the house, he saw Lily's red truck pull into the barnyard.

She dropped to the ground, staring at the barn. "Holy hell, Becket. What happened?" She didn't wait for his response, but ran for the water hose.

"I'll explain in a minute," he called out, barreling through the kitchen door. He slipped on something dark and wet and nearly fell. He straightened, and his heart sank to his knees. The liquid was blood, and a butcher knife lay against the baseboard with more blood streaked across the blade.

Becket ran straight for the phone in

the hallway. He knew he wouldn't find Kinsey in the house. Dillon had her. Sweet Jesus, he prayed she was still alive as he placed a call to 9-1-1. "There's been an attack at the Coyote Creek Ranch. Kinsey Phillips has been abducted. Send the sheriff, the National Guard, hell, call out anyone and everyone you can. Dillon Massey has her. He's insane and will kill her if we don't find her quickly. He'll probably head out of the county. And send the fire department to the Coyote Creek Ranch. The barn is on fire." He slammed the phone onto the cradle and ran back out the door.

Lily had the water hose aimed at the roof of the house, sweeping her arm right and left. The barn was too far gone to save. The best they could hope for was to prevent the other buildings from catching fire. But at that moment, Becket didn't give a damn about the barn or even the house.

"Where's Kinsey?" Lily asked.

His jaw tight, mind going in a million directions, Becket answered, "Massey has her."

"Damn." Lily redirected the hose to a burning ember that landed on a patch of

139

dried grass. "Where would he take her?"

That's the question that nagged him, and he had no good answers. "He'd be a fool to take her back to his house. That's the first place the police will look."

Another truck raced into the barnyard and came to a skidding, dusty stop. Chance leaped out. "Let me guess. Massey made his move. The bastard has to die." Chance pulled his personal protective gear from the back of his truck and pulled them on. "What are you waiting for?" He jabbed at finger in Becket's direction. "Find him. We'll take care of this."

"Nash will do his best to have road blocks set up to stop Massey," Lily assured Becket. "They'll find her."

"But will they find her in time? There's blood all over the kitchen." He swallowed over a dry throat. "I'm afraid he'll kill her."

"If he wasn't taking her back to his place, where would he go?"

Becket stood with his hands on his hips, trying to think like Massey. "The better question is: where would he go if he wanted to kill her?"

"Anywhere," Lily answered.

"He's mean enough to make her want to suffer," Becket said, forcing his mind to think like Massey. "The man was jealous about everything she loved. He took those things away to keep her tied to him."

"Kinsey came back to Hellfire," Lily said.

Becket's eyes widened. "Because it was the only home she'd ever known."

"But her parents are dead," Lily pointed out.

"He can't take away her memories—memories tied to the place she grew up. The place where her parents lived." Becket's heart pounded.

"You think he'd take her to the old Phillips' place?" Chance asked.

"Unless he's found on the road, it's the only other location he might have taken her." Becket's fists knotted. "He burned down this barn, he might try to destroy her house, as well."

Moving a few feet to her right, Lily nodded. "And she'd have nowhere to call home."

"Go," Chance said. "We're right

141

behind you as soon as the fire trucks arrive."

Becket ran for his truck.

"It's faster by horse!" Lily cried out.

She was right. By road, the drive would take fifteen minutes. But with all the tack burning in the barn, Becket would have to ride bareback, without a bridle.

His black gelding, Soot, pranced along the fence, whinnying, his eyes wild as the smoke blew his way.

Veering away from his truck, Becket vaulted the fence, snagged Soot by his halter, and swung up over his back. Then, leaning over the horse's neck, he twisted his hand in his mane and sank his heels into the animal's flanks.

Thankfully, the horse responded and leaped into a gallop, headed across the open pasture toward the old Phillips' place.

Becket prayed he'd get there in time. Already, he'd broken a promise to Kinsey. He'd said Dillon would never get his hands on her. When Becket caught up to the man, he would never do it again.

Chapter 8

When Kinsey woke, she lifted her head and stared around at her mother's piano and the sofa her parents had recovered for their twenty-fifth anniversary. For a moment she didn't understand why she was seeing these things, but then memories washed over her, and tears sprang to her eyes. She was in her parents' house. Sunshine streamed through dirty windows and dust motes spun in the air, but this was her home. The place she'd grown up. Pain throbbed in her forehead, and she tried to raise her hands to touch the spot, but they wouldn't move.

She sat in a dining room chair in the middle of the living room. Her wrists were secured to the arms of the chair with duct tape. A flash of movement drew her attention to the window overlooking the front yard.

Dillon stood outside, shaking a big red fuel can, slinging liquid across the front porch.

Then she smelled a pungent acrid scent, and her blood ran cold.

Kinsey strained and tugged at the bindings on her wrist. The tape held firm.

Dillon entered the house, reeking of gasoline and carrying the jug with him, splashing it across the floor.

"Dillon. Don't do this." She fought to keep a quaver from her voice. "I'll come home with you."

He snorted and slung more gasoline across the couch, some of it landing on his trouser legs. "I've tried to be reasonable."

Kinsey bit hard on her tongue. Now wasn't the time to tell him he was crazy and mean. "Take the tape off my wrists, Dillon. I'll go with you."

"I couldn't keep you away from this damn place, even after your parents died." He pulled a box of wooden matches from his pocket. "You had to come back, didn't you?"

"I only came to visit. I'm ready to go home now," she said, as calmly as she could, though her insides shook. With as much gasoline as he'd poured all over the room, it wouldn't take long to burn. She had to stop him before he lit a match. "Please, Dillon. Take me home. I promise not to leave you again."

"I could have forgiven you for leaving, but when I saw you kissing Grayson..." Dillon pulled a match from the box and stared at the red tip. "You always were a tease. I never trusted you around my teammates. I should have known you had something going on back here. Were you fucking the neighbor cowhand every time you came home to visit your parents?" He slid the match against the box and it ignited into a bright red-and-orange flame.

A gasp escaped. "Never, Dillon. I came home to see my parents. Only my parents."

"Shut up!" he yelled. "You're nothing but a lying bitch." Scowling, he flung the match.

Kinsey's breath caught as the match flew through the air and landed on the couch pushed up against the wall. The flame smoldered for a moment, then caught the gasoline and spread across the cushions.

Dillon's gaze followed the spread of the flame, his mouth curling into a smile.

"You love this place so much…you can stay and burn with it."

"Don't do this, Dillon. If you let me die in this house, you will have committed murder. Your football career will be over. You'll go to jail."

"And you will still be dead, and this house will be gone." He headed for the door. "My career is over, anyway. Coach wasn't playing me in the next game. Says I'm too much of a loose cannon." He kicked an end table, sending it flying across the room. "What the fuck does he know, anyway? Fuck him! Fuck you. And fuck this place. I'm done with it all."

Kinsey was so focused on the fire flaring in her old house, she almost didn't hear the hooves thundering against the ground until a horse slid to a stop outside, and a rider dropped to the ground.

"Kinsey!" A voice called out.

"Great." Dillon laughed. "I can take care of your lover at the same time." He grabbed another chair and slammed it against the dining table, breaking it into pieces. With one of the legs in his hand, he squared off opposite Becket as he charged through the door.

"Becket! Watch out!" Kinsey cried.

Dillon swung the sharp piece of wood.

Becket ducked, and the chair leg cracked against the doorframe. He hit Dillon with a hard punch to the gut.

Dillon doubled over, but came at Becket with a powerhouse swing, catching him across the chin.

Grunting, Becket jerked backward and fell out the door onto the porch.

Dillon followed, kicking at the man sprawled on the wooden deck.

In a flash, Becket caught Dillon's foot and twisted, sending him crashing against a wall, out of Kinsey's line of view.

She had other problems. Everywhere Dillon had spread the gasoline was in full flame and burning through the couch, the carpet, and into the wooden floors beneath. She bit back a coughing fit. If she didn't get out soon, she'd be engulfed by the flames.

Kinsey tried pounding the chair against the floor to break it, but the old chair held solid and refused to split. Flames spread across the floor, following the trail of gasoline to the door, blocking that exit. Now, the only direction clear of flames was toward the front picture window.

Outside the door, the men fought fiercely, grunting and banging against the outside walls. The front door slammed shut. Even if she made it through the flames, she couldn't reach the knob.

Kinsey braced her feet on the floor, leaned forward, and lifted the chair legs. Smoke stung her eyes, making them tear, and burned her lungs with each breath, but she wasn't ready to die.

She turned, aimed the legs of the chair at the window, and walked backward, picking up speed. If she didn't hit it hard enough, she wouldn't break the old glass. As she neared the window, she threw her entire body into the seat of the chair. The legs hit the window. Glass exploded outward, and she fell through, tucking her head to avoid the jagged edges.

The low windowsill caught the back of her legs, and she flipped over it, landing hard on the porch. The wooden chair back, taking the brunt of the landing, split into pieces.

Kinsey rolled across the shattered glass, the sharp edges cutting into her skin. She didn't care. Cuts and bruises would heal—she had proof of that fact. If she didn't get completely away from the house, her dive through the window wouldn't have helped. Still attached to the arms and back of the chair, but with the legs broken off, she struggled to get her feet beneath her.

On the other end of the porch, Dillon had pinned down Becket and pummeled his face.

"Leave him alone!" Kinsey screamed.

Dillon's head shot up, and he glared at her. He stopped hitting Becket and staggered to his feet, blood dripping from his nose and where she'd stabbed him in the arm and thigh. One eye was swelling, and a jagged wound cut across his eyebrow. "No fucking way!" Dillon shouted. "You can't leave."

The fire had spread inside the house, catching on the curtains around the broken window. A flaming ember wafted out onto the porch, igniting the gasoline Dillon had sluiced over the weathered boards.

A breeze fanned the flame, making it shoot up as Dillon plowed through. His trousers caught on fire, the flames rising up his leg.

Kinsey managed to get to her feet and braced herself for the pending impact.

Before Dillon reached Kinsey, Becket grabbed him from behind, his hands hard on the football player's shoulders.

Dillon roared and fought to free his arms from Becket's hold, the fire creeping up the front of his pants.

Unable to contain the bigger man for long, Becket shoved him sideways, away from Kinsey.

Dillon fell through the broken window into the burning house.

Flames spread across the porch toward Kinsey.

Becket ran for her, scooped her into his arms, chair parts and all, and leaped off the porch. When he landed, his legs buckled beneath him, and they rolled across the ground, away from the flaming house.

Becket pushed to a sitting position and helped her up to one as well. "Are you all right?" He rested his hands on her shoulders and searched her face, his brows pulled into a frown.

Cut, bruised, and bleeding, she found the energy to smile. "I'm alive."

He captured her face in his hands and gave her a quick, hard kiss on the lips, then unwound the duct tape from one of her wrists and what was left of the arms and back of the chair. When the tape reached her bare skin, he eased the adhesive loose. Once one wrist was free, he kissed her red skin. "Can you manage the rest?"

Blood pounding in her ears, she nodded.

"I'm going after Dillon." He got up and helped her to her feet.

Kinsey touched his arm. "Be careful." If the fire didn't hurt Becket, Dillon might still have enough energy to knock him out.

Without protective clothing, Becket risked his own life going into the burning house.

Heart lodged in her throat, she worked the tape loose with her fingers while tracking Becket's progress.

She prayed he'd come out of it alive.

Now that she'd found him again, she wanted him to stick around long enough to make him fall in love with her. She was well on her way to being head over heels for him.

As Kinsey shook free of the old chair, she saw Becket kick open the front door and run inside.

With his shirt pulled up over his nostrils, Becket entered the house, running through the line of fire, dodging the hot spots. Massey had used an accelerant, gasoline from the smell of it, to ignite the building. Though he'd gone through the window, landing inside the living room, the man was nowhere to be seen.

"Massey!" he yelled, and then coughed, smoke burning the lining of his lungs and the heat making breathing equally hard.

Besides the roar of the fire, no other sound came to him. Throwing an arm over his head and ducking low, he ran through the burning house into the kitchen. The door leading out the back of the house stood wide open.

Damn. He'd gone out the back. Which meant he could have rounded to the front by now.

Kinsey.

Becket spun, intending to take the shortest route through the house, but the fire had intensified in the living room, having spread to the ceiling. Timbers crashed down, shooting sparks into the air.

Going back the way he'd come was no longer an option. He had to get to Kinsey. Fast.

Bolting for the back door, he leaped off the porch. The sound of sirens rang out across the countryside as Becket ran around the side of the burning structure. When he reached the front yard, he ground to a halt and his heart stopped.

Massey had Kinsey from behind, his arm looped around her neck in a chokehold.

Her face was blue, turning bluer by the moment.

"Let her go, Massey." Pulse pounding against his eardrums, Becket inched toward them. "It's over."

Kinsey scratched at Massey's arms,

fighting for breath. Fighting for her life.

"Back off, or I'll kill her."

"Yeah. You've already proved you'd kill her anyway." Becket considered his options. He could charge the two. He'd hit Kinsey first, but if he could knock them both over, Massey might loosen his chokehold. If he did nothing, Massey would kill her anyway.

Bunching his muscles, Becket raced toward Kinsey. At the same time, he saw her hand rise to Massey's face.

She jammed her thumb into his eye.

Massey screamed and loosened his hold.

Kinsey jammed her elbow into his gut.

Dillon let go, she dropped to the ground and rolled to the side as Becket plowed into Massey, slamming him up against a tree.

The man's head hit with a loud crack, and he slumped to the ground.

A fire truck rolled down the driveway as Becket helped Kinsey to her feet and held her in the curve of his arms. "I'm sorry."

"Why are you sorry?" she asked, her voice gravelly. "If you hadn't come around when you did, Dillon would have killed me."

"If I had stayed put, I could have kept him from getting to you."

"You're a good man, Becket. You wouldn't leave your worst enemy in that fire." She faced him, lacing her hands in the hair at the nape of his neck. "That's what I love about you."

His arms circled her waist, and he pulled her to him. "There are a lot of things I love about you. But all those scratches and bruises need to be tended to first."

Firefighters converged on the house, and paramedics surrounded Kinsey, Becket, and Massey.

Massey was loaded into an ambulance and taken away.

The paramedics treated Kinsey's wounds and checked both her and Becket for signs of a concussion.

A second ambulance pulled up. The paramedic opened the door and started to pull out the gurney.

"We can walk," Kinsey insisted.

"Though I didn't seen signs of concussion, you both should be checked over by a doctor, just to be safe," the paramedic said

Kinsey looked to Becket. "I won't go unless he comes with me in the ambulance."

"You're not going anywhere near Massey without me." Becket stood with hands on his hips.

She lifted a shoulder and smiled. "Then I guess we're both going to the hospital."

Inside the ambulance, Kinsey and Becket sat beside each other on the gurney. The paramedic insisted they both wear oxygen masks during the drive, which precluded talking.

Kinsey slipped her hand in his and rode all the way to the trauma center in Hellfire.

The doctor checked them out and cleared them to go home.

"What about Dillon?" Kinsey asked.

The doctor's brows dipped. "Are you a relative?"

Kinsey shook her head.

"I'm sorry, I can't share that information."

On the way out of the examination room, Becket could see into the next room. Nurses and a doctor worked over Massey.

Nash, dressed in his sheriff's deputy uniform, met them in the reception area. "Are you two going to live?"

Becket hugged Kinsey to him, careful not to touch her bandages and bruises. "We will. As long as Massey isn't let loose on the street."

"We have so many charges compiled against him, he's not going anywhere but the state penitentiary."

Kinsey pressed into Becket's side. "Good."

"I'll see you two back at the house. Chance and Rider are finishing up at the old Phillips' place. There won't be anything to salvage." He touched Kinsey's arm. "I'm sorry."

Becket ran his hand up and down her arm, knowing what she must be feeling.

She nodded, her eyes awash with tears.

Nash turned to Becket. "Lily's

157

waiting outside."

"What about the barn at our ranch?" Becket queried, although he wasn't holding out much hope.

Nash shook his head. "Gone. Thankfully, all other buildings are intact. Even though the barn burned to the ground, keep in mind, buildings can be replaced. People can't. I'm glad you and Kinsey are okay."

Becket hugged his brother. "Me, too."

Nash turned to Kinsey and hugged her.

"Thanks." Kinsey hugged him back. "You're right. I'd rather lose the house and barn than you, Becket, or any of your siblings."

Nash nodded and stepped past them to speak with the doctor.

"Come on." Becket turned with her in the circle of his arm and walked toward the exit. "Let's go home."

She snuggled against him, her arm around his middle. "I promise to get a place of my own as soon as I can get a job and save up the necessary deposits."

"You have a place to live for as long as you like," Becket said, his voice gruffer than he'd intended. "Forever, if things work out."

She slowed to a stop and faced him. "How's that?"

Maybe he was pushing things too fast, but he'd almost lost her that day. "None of us know how long we have on this earth."

Her brows twisted. "I'm not following."

"I'm just saying, I don't want to waste time." He held both of her hands and squeezed. "After you have a chance to recover, you and I are going out on a date. A real date."

"I'd like that."

"We could take it slow," he continued, running a thumb over her knuckles. "Just dinner. Maybe a movie, and end it with a kiss, if you want."

She eased from his grip, and a hand settled on his chest. "What if I don't?"

His heart stuttered, and he captured her hand in his. God, if she walked away from him now, he didn't know what he'd do. This woman had the potential to be the one to restore his faith in women. To remind him what love was all about, and the sacrifices he'd willingly make to keep her safe and happy.

Becket raised her hand to his lips, pressing a kiss into her palm. "Kinsey, you're free to choose who you want to be with. I will never force you to do anything you don't want to do."

"I know." She cupped his cheek. "What I meant is: what if I don't want just a kiss?" Leaning up on her toes, she brushed her lips across his, and then whispered in his ear, "What if I want more? What if I want to ride out in a pasture on a four-wheeler with you?"

His heart exploded with joy, and he wrapped her in his arms, rubbing his cheek against her hair. "Sweetheart, if you asked me to ride you to the moon and back, I'd be happy to take you. You name it. I'm there."

"Take me home, cowboy. I think doing it in a bed this time would be nice."

"Are you sure?" He stared down at her, his gaze taking in the myriad bandages covering her arms and legs. "You're a mess."

"I've never been more certain in my entire life. And you're pretty beat up yourself." She touched her fingertip to the black eye he'd earned in his fight with Massey. "I'm sorry you had to get involved in my screwed-up life."

"I wouldn't have it any other way." Becket grinned. "A few bumps and bruises, I can live with. So, if you're sure...I'm sure."

She laughed and swept an arm toward the exit. "Home, it is."

As they left the trauma clinic, Becket swept Kinsey off her feet and carried her toward Lily's waiting truck.

She laughed, wrapped her arms around his neck, and nuzzled his ear. "I think I could fall in love with you."

He stopped and smiled down into her happy face. "Sweetheart, I'm well on my way there, myself." Then he kissed her soundly, ignoring the stares of his sister and the people who had to step around him to enter the building.

Love didn't take a week, a month, or a year to develop. Sometimes love took a minute, an hour, a day, or a look. He'd give her the space she needed to recover. But the fire in his heart would burn eternal for this woman and, if she let him, he would spend a lifetime proving it.

THE END

About the Author

ELLE JAMES also writing as MYLA JACKSON is a *New York Times* and *USA Today* Bestselling author of books including cowboys, intrigues and paranormal adventures that keep her readers on the edges of their seats. With over eighty works in a variety of sub-genres and lengths she has published with Harlequin, Samhain, Ellora's Cave, Kensington, Cleis Press, and Avon. When she's not at her computer, she's traveling, snow-skiing, boating, or riding her ATV, dreaming up new stories. Learn more about Elle James at www.ellejames.com

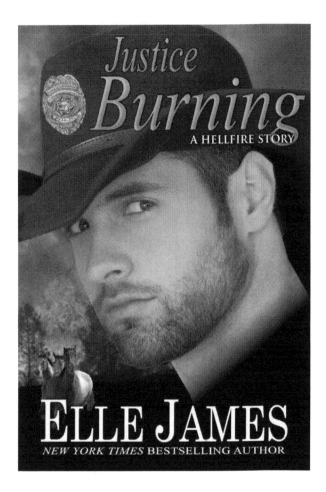

Justice
Burning
A HELLFIRE STORY

ELLE JAMES
NEW YORK TIMES BESTSELLING AUTHOR

Justice Burning

HELLFIRE SERIES

BOOK #2

ELLE JAMES

New York Times & USA Today
Bestselling Author

Chapter 1

"THE BASTARD!" Phoebe Sinclair's usual easy-going demeanor had taken a major hit. She checked the rearview mirror, couldn't see anything past the train of her wedding dress flying out behind her. When she'd discovered her fiancé had skipped out on the wedding just seconds before she was due to walk down the aisle, she'd practically jumped into the convertible. He'd left the church, no explanation, no excuses. Which meant Phoebe would have had to face her parents and their guests to break the news alone. There wouldn't be a wedding. The groom had run out on her.

Jilted.

Never mind she'd already been having extremely cold feet. Two hours earlier, she'd been a nervous bride, convinced she was making a huge mistake by marrying a man her father had selected as perfect husband material for his darling daughter. Her mother had argued that Ryan would help elevate her social status even more. Not that Phoebe cared two hoots about status.

Phoebe, the dutiful daughter who'd always done what her parents wanted, who never had anxiety issues, could have used one of her mother's anti-anxiety pills. On the very verge of walking down the aisle of the church to promise to love, honor and cherish Ryan Bratton, a colleague of her father's, she'd asked herself *why?* Why was she marrying a man with whom she didn't have much in common? Why was she allowing her parents to choose her husband? Why had she let herself be swept into the whole wedding experience?

The pathetic answer was that all of her Dallas debutante friends were either engaged or married. Some were pregnant with their first babies.

Tick tock, tick tock.

Her damned biological clock had been ticking pretty darned loud when her father proclaimed it was time to get married and produce heirs. He wasn't getting any younger and he wanted to know he'd have someone to pass the oil speculation business to when he was gone.

Phoebe slowed behind a tractor hauling a large round hay bale. Wisps of straw flew over the top of the convertible's windshield, tangling in her hair. Swerving toward the center of the road, she peered around the big green John Deere. The lane was clear and she sped past.

Her father could sell the damned business for all she cared. Phoebe had never had a head for business, preferring to hang out with the horses on their ranch. She hadn't really been that interested in dating, finding most of the men in her parents' circle either old like her father, greedy or lazy. When she went out on dates, many of the men were more interested in her father's assets than in her own.

She'd stared into the full-length mirror, her heart pounding, perspiration popping out on her forehead and upper lip, after her mother had applied makeup to her face. Phoebe couldn't do it. She didn't love Ryan. Though her father thought highly of him, his opinion of Ryan wasn't enough.

Sure, he'd had her grandmother's locket professionally reworked by a jeweler, with a brand new chain and a picture of her grandmother inside. The extremely thoughtful gift had almost convinced her he was the man she needed. But standing in front of the mirror, staring at the stranger in the white dress, about to marry a man she really didn't know, she'd started into a full-on panic attack.

Her mother had entered the room, slapped a paper bag into her hand and told her to breathe into the bag. Then her mother had straightened her veil, patted powder on her face and turned her toward the door with a parting comment, "Don't embarrass me." Her mother moved inside the sanctuary to take her seat.

Phoebe stood outside the door, waiting for the cue for her bridesmaids to make the long trip down the aisle ahead of her. Something had held up the ceremony. Five minutes turned to ten but her cue didn't come.

One of the groomsmen ducked out of the sanctuary, spotted her and waved her back toward the anterooms.

Phoebe handed her bouquet to her maid of honor, a silly society girl her mother had chosen since Phoebe didn't have many girlfriends suitable to wear the ridiculous bridesmaid gowns. "I'll be a moment." Phoebe hurriedly joined the groomsman.

He glanced over her shoulder at the others watching and then leaned close to whisper, "We have a problem."

Her heart had fluttered, her stomach roiling. "What's wrong?"

The man tugged at his collar as if the tie constricted his vocal cords.

Phoebe wanted to take a hold of the tie and tug on it herself. Hard. "Spit it out," she finally said.

He took a deep breath and blurted, "Ryan disappeared."

"What?" And her mother had been afraid *Phoebe* would embarrass her. "He ran out? Did he say anything before he disappeared?"

The young man's face turned a bright red and he shook his head.

"You have got to be kidding." Surely Ryan had only gone to the restroom or outside to catch a breath of fresh air. Phoebe stormed off toward the room the groom was supposed to use for wedding preparations. Flinging open the door, she marched in. "Ryan, you better get your scrawny ass up to the altar…"

The room was empty. Ryan and his tuxedo were gone.

"Really?" she cried. "*You* got cold feet?" Blood pounded in her ears. She stared around the room, hoping he was hiding somewhere and going to spring out and say *surprise!*

With a sanctuary full of five hundred of her parents' closest friends waiting for the wedding to start, Phoebe didn't know what to do. She'd agreed to marry Ryan, not because she particularly loved him, but because no one else had come along in her thirty-one years who inspired the soul-defining passion she had expected to come with falling in love. Ryan could kiss okay and he'd tried to please her when they'd been more intimate. Still…nothing. No sparks, no earth-shaking anything. Surely all those romance novels she'd read late into the night weren't all pure fantasy.

Phoebe had begun to think she didn't have the romantic gene in her body, so she'd settled for Ryan. Now, he'd skipped out. Jilted her at the altar and left her with the task of telling all the five hundred strangers her fiancé hadn't wanted to marry her after all. "I could kill him," she said.

"Excuse me?" a voice said behind her.

With a little scream, she spun to face Ryan's best man, Warren Ledbetter. "Did you know he was thinking of backing out of this circus of a wedding?" she demanded.

He shook his head. "He told me to go on to the sanctuary, that he'd be there momentarily. That was fifteen minutes ago."

"Well, I'm not telling all those people this event isn't happening." She waved a hand toward the church. "I'm not taking the rap for it. My father and mother will be livid after spending a small fortune on this show."

Warren's eyes widened. "What are you going to do?"

"I don't know." She glanced around the room and over her shoulder at the hallway. The choice had come down to either face her parents and the sanctuary full of people, or leave and hoping her parents didn't hate her for eternity.

Phoebe's feet, in the white satin pumps, took her toward the door. When the dutiful daughter should have turned left to go to the sanctuary, she turned right. Rather than face her parents, Phoebe opted to run. Yes, leaving was the coward's way out, but she'd had enough of her parents running her life, choosing her clothes, her friends and her husband.

She'd run out the side door of the church nursery to a playground where she hurried past the swings and play fort. Out in the Texas sunshine, she lifted her skirts and ran, breathing in the fresh taste of freedom. If Ryan could skip out of a wedding neither of them really wanted, so could she.

Phoebe dared to dream of a life she chose to live. She could get a job, pay her own way, make her own friends and really live. The faster she ran, the better she felt until she kicked off her heels and sprinted toward the parking lot out front.

Before she reached it, Phoebe ground to a stop. She'd arrived in her parents' chauffeur-driven town car. The church was off the usual routes of taxi drivers, and she didn't have any money to pay a driver. Nor did she have a cell phone to call for a pick up. Her newfound freedom took a turn for the worst.

Then she spied the wedding car, a sleek black Cadillac convertible with specially decorated cans tied with silk ribbons beneath the bumper, parked outside the door to the church's banquet hall where the reception was to be held after the wedding. A banner affixed to the trunk read JUST MARRIED. Daring to hope, she inched up to the driver's side of the vehicle and looked inside.

Hope flared in her chest at the sight of the keys in the ignition.

Gathering her skirts, she jumped in, twisted the key and drove away from the church, leaving behind what would be her disappointed, embarrassed parents and a life she never seemed to fit into.

Thus started the great adventure.

Phoebe wore a wedding dress, didn't have a penny tucked away on any part of her body, and had taken her fiancé's convertible. Not until she'd left Dallas and put over a hundred miles between her and the wedding guests did the adrenaline wear off. She could be charged with grand theft auto. The car belonged to her delinquent fiancé, not her. At the moment that thought struck, she swerved to the side of the road and bumped over some trash on the shoulder. Her heart raced, and she tried to think. She could ditch the car and call the police to tell them where they could find it. Or she could just ditch the car in some backwater town and...and...what?

She couldn't steal another. Without a dollar on her, she couldn't buy a bus ticket or a rent a car. Damn. She should have thought this escape through a little more thoroughly. One thing was certain, she couldn't stay on the side of the road. A sign a few miles back indicated a town was coming up. What was the name? Hellfire? A peculiar name for a town.

Her stomach rumbled, reminding her she hadn't eaten since the night before. Maybe she could stop there, find a job and work for food. With a little bit of a plan in mind, she drove toward the town. She hadn't gone more than a quarter of a mile when a sharp pop sounded, and the car pulled to the right.

Phoebe steered off the road and got out. Wadding up her skirt, she folded it over her arm and padded around the front of the car, gravel and grass digging into her tender bare feet. As she'd suspected, the right front tire was flat. Great. Her shoulders slumped. She'd never changed a flat tire in her life and her father had never demonstrated the process. He'd whip out his cell phone, call for roadside assistance and wait until help arrived. Phoebe didn't have that luxury, with neither a cell phone, nor a roadside assistance service that didn't belong to her daddy. Not to mention, that wasn't what independent women did. How the hell did one change a flat tire?

She walked back around to the driver's side and pulled the keys from the ignition. When she'd seen movies where the characters had to change a tire, they always went to the trunk. The spare tire should be in the trunk. It stood to reason, the tools to change the flat would be in the trunk as well. Keys in hand, she walked to the back of the vehicle, and hit the button to pop open the trunk.

With her dress in hand, barefooted, broke and determined, she leaned over and studied the space. A blanket lay across a rather large lump in the back. Hopefully the spare tire. Phoebe grabbed the blanket and yanked it off.

She gasped and staggered backward, all the blood draining from her head. This couldn't be happening. *No. No. No.* Phoebe pressed her hand to her lips and edged closer to look again, praying she'd imagined what she'd seen.

Nope.

The lump beneath the blanket was none other than her missing groom, Ryan. Based on his waxy gray face and open eyes staring at nothing, the man was well and truly dead.

Sweet Jesus. Oh, sweet Jesus. Phoebe bit down on her bottom lip. Had she checked the trunk before she'd gone one hundred miles, would he have been alive enough to resuscitate? She gulped. Had she killed him by not checking? Though she hadn't really loved him, she never wished him dead.

The next thought hit her square in

the gut. She'd stolen Ryan's car, run out on the wedding, and now had his dead body in the back of the vehicle. To make it worse, she had a witness who could state he heard her say, *I'll kill him.* The best man had been there when she'd gone to find Ryan.

When the cops caught up with her and Ryan's car, they'd find his body, receive testimony from his best man and presume Phoebe had killed him. Her independence would come to a screeching halt when she was arrested, booked and thrown in jail for the rest of her life.

Her head spinning, Phoebe stood back, looking around at the rolling grasslands. Not a car was in sight. She couldn't just walk away. Barefoot, no telling how far to the nearest town, she wouldn't make it. Phoebe hadn't planned to start a new life on the lam for a murder she didn't commit.

Scrambling for something, *anything,* she could do to get out of the mess she'd landed in, she slammed the trunk, hurried around the car and jumped into the driver's seat. The wind chose that moment to pick up and her dress billowed around her as she pulled forward on the flat tire, bumping along the shoulder of the road. Her skirt flew up in her face. Trying to flatten it so that she could see, she shifted her foot to hit the brake, but she hit the accelerator instead. The convertible leaped forward, ran off the road and slammed into a fence post, throwing Phoebe forward, banging her forehead against the steering wheel. She saw stars that quickly changed to bright blue strobes. As her vision cleared, she realized the lights were attached to a police vehicle.

Could her day get any worse?

"Unit 470, we have a report of some teenagers drag racing on farm to market road 476 at the old Dunwitty grain silo."

"10-4." Deputy Nash Grayson slowed the sheriff's deputy SUV, checked the road ahead leading into Hellfire, and glanced in his rearview mirror. No one coming. No one going. Quiet, placid, small-town Texas, where nothing much happened. He made a U-turn and headed back out into the countryside.

Thirteen months ago, he'd been in full combat gear, slipping through the streets of a small village in Afghanistan, searching for Taliban rebels. His fourth tour to the Middle East, he knew the drill. Kill the bad guys, not the civilians.

The nation he was sworn to defend didn't understand how difficult it was to tell the difference. A smiling Afghan approaching a checkpoint might have explosives strapped to his waist beneath the robe he wore. Or a mother might send her child armed with a grenade into a group of soldiers visiting an orphanage. Over there, he had to remain vigilant. Hell, he'd needed eyes in the back of his head. Always alert, always listening and looking for sudden movement.

After a year back in his hometown of Hellfire, he still jumped at loud noises and dropped into a fighting stance when someone sneaked up behind him. But the bucolic life of the small town had helped him learn to breathe deeply again. Well, not too deeply when the wind blew from the direction of the local stockyard. The stench of cattle crap and urine filled the air on those days.

Other than the usual teenaged

hijinks and an occasional domestic quarrel, things were pretty laid back. Almost too much so. Thankfully, when he wasn't on the job, Nash had the family ranch to retreat to. There, he could work with the animals and burn off some of his restless energy.

Although he was nearing the end of his shift, Nash didn't mind checking out the drag racing report. A typical Saturday in the country. Hellfire didn't have a bowling alley or movie theater. The only organized activities available to the kids were football and rodeo. High school football games drew everyone out on Friday evenings in the fall. Which left Saturday and Sunday to do chores before the kids returned to school and parents to work on Monday. But after chores, the teens liked to gather at the town's only fast food drive-in or find a place to raise hell out in the countryside. Everything from cow-tipping to mud-riding in the bottoms.

Today's hell-raising just happened to be drag racing.

Nash pulled into the rutted gravel road leading to the abandoned Dunwitty silos. Apparently, the race was in full swing, because all eyes were on the vehicles at the center of the mob. Two tricked-out trucks, with knobby tires and fat chrome exhaust pipes, shot out of the crowd of young people and barreled along the wide gravel road running half a mile in length. Their engines rumbled, the sound reverberating through the warm, late-afternoon air.

Guys in jeans, cowboy boots and hats punched the air, whooping and hollering. Girls in frayed cutoffs and shirts tied at their midriffs, laughed and screamed for the drivers to go faster.

Nothing Nash could do at that point would slow the racing trucks. If he didn't know they were trespassing, he'd enjoy the race and then slip away before anyone was the wiser about his presence there.

But this was Dunwitty's place and the clearly posted NO TRESPASSING signs out front were all the rules Nash needed. He followed the rules, the structure of his job and his life giving him comfort.

When the trucks reached the end of the road, the crowd of young people shouted, yelled, hooted and whistled for the winner. The trucks turned around and drove back to the silos, stopping as the kids converged on them.

Nash got out of his vehicle. Time to spoil the fun.

One young man, Johnny Austin, spotted Nash before he reached the edge of the crowd. "Time to leave," he shouted, loud enough to be heard over the noise of the celebration.

All faces turned toward him.

With a wave, Nash jerked his head toward the silos. "Sorry, folks. I gotta break it up. You're trespassing."

"Aw," the group said as a collective.

The guys and girls piled into the cars and trucks and filed out of the silo area, one by one.

Once they'd all gone, Nash climbed into his SUV and headed back to town to hang up his hat and go home. Another day, another dollar. The excitement was killing him. He chuckled. He'd thought about going to work in Houston, where a shooting occurred every day. Maybe more. But he liked being near the ranch, the horses and cattle. He'd missed it when he'd been on active duty.

Perhaps he needed a woman in his life. Like his brother Becket, who'd never been happier. Up until Kinsey had come back into his brother's life, Nash had been content to be a bachelor. Seeing them together, always touching and kissing…Never mind the headboard banging and springs squeaking into the wee hours of the morning. Nash had gone so far as to sleep in the barn a few times, or asked for the night shift to avoid the happy copulating going on in the ranch house master bedroom.

Yeah, Houston was looking more and more like a possibility.

Ahead, he spied a strange sight. A shiny black convertible, with cans strung out behind and a banner proclaiming JUST MARRIED, sped toward town, weaving side to side, white fabric ballooning up from the driver's seat like a parachute.

His interest spiked, and he increased his speed, hoping to catch up to the car to check it out.

Other Titles
by Elle James

Alaskan Fantasy
Blown Away
Cowboy Sanctuary
Lakota Baby
Dakota Meltdown
Beneath the Texas Moon